Praise for *Fox Season and Other Short Stories*

"Dale is between cultures, rooted in one, integrated into another, perfectly placed as observer and participant. She writes with an entrancing blend of distance and intimacy. In this country, she is an immigrant, but one who knows us and our language too well for comfort. Reading her, it feels that someone who has learned to be one of us, now does it better than we do. She knows what makes us laugh, and what makes us laughable."
—Jeremy Hardy, comedian

"Agnieszka Dale's impressive debut depicts on a large canvas our current world of chaos. Her sharp, humorous, sensitive and metaphorical style confirms that a new, exciting voice has arrived on the scene."
—Xiaolu Guo, author of *A Concise Chinese-English Dictionary for Lovers*, nominated for 2007 Orange Prize for Fiction

"Agnieszka Dale's psychological territory is bridge-building. She straddles the land of her birth—Poland—and her adoptive UK home. National shape-shifting and the individual's pliability in reconciling the personal and the communal are the underpinnings of her work; she takes to them with gusto."
—John Munch, *Riveting Reviews*, *European Literature Network*

"Be very careful when reading Agnieszka Dale's book, because her stories are memorable and have the perverse power to redefine concepts such as identity, nation, immigration, and homeland. They can change your whole perspective on the world. A most intriguing debut!"
—Wioletta Greg, author of *Swallowing Mercury*, longlisted for 2017 Booker International Prize

"Agnieszka Dale writes stories about outsiders. Separated by nationality, and by their ability to think, and their ability to *feel*—their tales from a Polish perspective are fired by political urgency, but they are also tender, wise, disturbing and very, very funny. Dale nimbly darts between naturalism and absurdism, between domestic drama and science fiction, all to bewitching effect."

—Robert Shearman, 2010 British Fantasy Award winner for his collection *Love Songs for the Shy and Cynical*; *Doctor Who* writer

"Agnieszka Dale writes with passion and wit. Her stories can be achingly specific and, at times, so big and so fundamental that they achieve the quality of myths."

—Paul Maliszewski, author of *Prayer and Parable*

"Funny, moving, inventive stories by a young writer worth waiting for on the other side of Brexit."

—Scott Bradfield, author of *Animal Planet*

"These fictions are a constant delight, with enigmatic depths beneath the sparkling prose. By turns tender and playful, the stories are the work of a unique imagination."

—Aiden O'Reilly, author of *Greetings, Hero*

"*Fox Season* by Agnieszka Dale needs to be read slowly. Give each of the twenty-one stories in this collection—some touching, some disturbing, all intelligent—your full attention, for they deserve it. There are depths here: dark currents of meaning flowing beneath what may appear to be a calm and simple surface. Most impressive!"

—John Ravenscroft, author of *Fishing for Jasmine*

Fox
Season

and Other Short Stories

Agnieszka Dale

Jantar Publishing
London 2017

First published in London, Great Britain in 2017 by
Jantar Publishing Ltd
www.jantarpublishing.com

Agnieszka Dale
Fox Season and Other Short Stories
All rights reserved

Text © Agnieszka Dale
Cover and book design by Jack Coling

"Peek-a-boo" was originally published in the 2011 Fine Line short story collection *Even Birds Are Chained to the Sky*. "Belgian Passion" was originally selected for Liars' League London in February 2013. "Fox Season" was broadcast on BBC Radio 4 on 11 September, 2015. A version of "A Happy Nation" was broadcast on BBC Radio 4 on 14 October, 2016.

The right of Agnieszka Dale to be identified as author of this work has been asserted in accordance with sections 77 and 78 of the Copyright and Patents Act 1988.

All persons in this collection are fictitious. All emotions are true.

A CIP catalogue record for this book is available from the British Library.
ISBN 978-0-9933773-1-0

Printed and bound in the Czech Republic by EUROPRINT a.s.

To Hannah and Stan

Contents

Peek-a-boo

Maja was conceived during the spin cycle of our Hotpoint WT965 twenty-one months ago. When I left her at the nursery this morning—our first day apart—I could not stop sobbing. Now I want to see her again.

My left nipple is stone hard. I go to the toilet to express some milk. More milk comes into my breasts. But it doesn't flow out. They say a picture of your baby can help you to relax. I haven't got any with me. I look at the photo of the first scan that I keep in my wallet. My little Maja, the size of a hand, is blowing raspberries at us, or waving. Although the midwife had said "baby" was scratching its nose. If only the nursery staff were as helpful as midwives. But once the child is born, nobody gives a damn, it seems.

The picture of the first scan does not do the trick. If only I could find a way to sign into Skype. I try again and again but my browser crashes every time. My stomach feels like a washing machine spinning at 1000 rpm. Don't get me wrong. I like my washing machine. It's my favourite domestic appliance. We used to make love on top of it, but now that I'm a mother, a bed seems more appropriate.

It seems odd to be back at my desk. The other mothers look me up and down to check if my stomach has gone back to its original size. The men look at my enlarged bosom. It feels intrusive. Do they also want to know if the sexual relations with my partner have returned to normal? How can anything ever be normal again? I call the helpdesk and ask if they could assist me. The man on the other side—I think his name is Adam—agrees a bit too readily. Is it because he thinks I'm a yummy mummy or he finds me disgustingly mumsy and wants to get rid of me?

"Your computer account has been locked out," he says. "There are countless sites on the Internet with cameras pointed at virtually everything. A lot of them are porn sites. You're not allowed to use Skype at work, I'm afraid." His voice is sweaty like he's in the middle of watching a peep show. He sounds Slovakian in the way he rolls his *r*'s when pronouncing "porn."

"*Kurwa mać!*" I swear more now that I'm a mother.

Adam laughs.

"Polish?"

"*Tak.*"

He logs me in.

Here is Maja. I can only see her feet and arms as Sarah, to whom I handed Maja over this morning, obstructs everything else. She looks like a former prison guard. I wave to Maja but she does not see me. Here is Mummy, I say. Look at Mummy. Mummy can see you. She is eating a piece of apple and playing with her shoe. They really should not let her eat and touch her shoe at the same time. The shoe is mucky, Maja. Put it away, please. She is no longer wearing her socks inside her shoes. She will have blisters on her feet! Before I can see any blisters, the video stream starts breaking and my computer crashes.

I try to sign in again but my Skype crashes every time I do it. I call the nursery.

"Could you please put the socks back on Maja's feet," I say.

"But she's very unhappy with her socks on," says Sarah.

A short silence follows.

"Put the bloody socks on," I say, my stomach turning at 1200 rpm. Before she can answer back, I put the phone down.

I call Adam and explain my computer problem.

He logs me back in, remotely. A rinse cycle kicks in and I manage to relax a little.

"One more time, and you'll have to pay me," he says.

"How much?"

"It's not about money," he says.

Sarah has finally moved, too, and I can see Maja. She turns her head to the left and looks me straight in the eye. My left breast starts filling up with milk even more, until it feels like a full bladder. I put my nose against the screen and wave to her. She giggles and waves back. She comes closer to the camera and turns her head to the left. I slowly lift up my shirt and put the breast against the screen. She opens her mouth and latches on.

My brain is melting. I feel like a giant soft toy, a teddy with a bosom…

After a minute or two, Maja unlatches. I sit back.

"Could you restart your computer for me, please?" says Adam. His looks match his voice. He is cross-eyed.

I look down at my shirt. It's got two wet patches. Maja is gone. It's midday and she's having her nap now. At home we would be cuddled up together on the sofa, snoozing, with the washing machine finishing its first song of the day.

I sneak out of work three minutes early, at three minutes to four. There is no need to rush to get my train but a casual stroll seems wrong without a pushchair. I run to the station and then wait on the platform for ten minutes. I check the train schedule several times. Mummy is coming, Maja, Mummy is on her way.

By the time my train arrives, the tips of my fingernails are all chewed.

We stop at Crystal Palace for a good five minutes. I look at the long grass in between the unused railway tracks. Either its length or the fact that it's growing so randomly in a public place reminds me of home, where there are still bits of grass growing freely.

Over ten years ago, my then-boyfriend said that he would like me not to shave my armpits for a while, as it would remind him of another place.

"You want me to have a fanny under each armpit? That makes two fannies. Three if you count the other place."

He got cross with me. A month later we broke up. He was a dentist from Kraków in his thirties while I was a twenty-two-year-old student from Warsaw. I still think, how odd he did not laugh. What a freak. Erik would laugh.

I get off at Forest Hill. It's only been forty-five minutes since I last went to a toilet but I need to go again.

"Sorry, Milka, the toilets are locked. We're having a drainage problem," says Trish, a French Canadian acquaintance of mine. She owns the pub next to the station. I know her from my birthing classes at Guy's Hospital.

"No worries, I think I can hold on for a few more minutes. How is your bump?" I ask. She looks better in her second pregnancy but I don't tell her that. I know what she will say: "It's because this time it's a boy. Daughters take away a mother's good looks and boys bring them back."

"My bump is fine but I hate not seeing a doctor in my pregnancy. Women, women everywhere. I wish there was a *midhusband* of some sort that I could see," she scratches her bump as if it was a buttock.

I nod. It is better not to mess with pregnant women. They can be aggressive.

"In Canada, midwives are much more helpful," she says. For Trish, everything is better in North America. That's where she gave birth to her daughter. She was highly medicated during the delivery. High on gas 'n' air, she was dancing to rock 'n' roll.

The nursery is only two minutes up the road and I tell myself, you can do it, you can hold on for a few more minutes. It reminds me of the point of delivery when I had to push Maja out, only now it's the opposite; I need to push in, keep things inside me. I can't decide which is worse.

Finally, through the window, I can see Maja playing with a teddy. Both of my breasts start filling up with milk. How much more milk can they fit in? I'm about to be drowned by all the liquids produced by my own body. The inside of my stomach is sweating and I can't even wipe that sweat off. It's like laundry taken out of a tumble drier after five minutes, still damp, but hot. As soon as Maja sees me, she starts crying.

"Did she have a good day?" I shout to Sarah but she can't hear me. Maja screams louder and louder as if I wasn't her mother but an abductor. I give her a big hug but that does not help. I sniff her bottom through her Mothercare baby jeans and say to Sarah: "I think that she needs her nappy changing." I then sniff Maja's head. It smells of another woman's perfume. I rush into a nappy changing room and close the doors behind me. Maja gives me a big smile. I smile back.

"I missed you so much today," I say.

Maja giggles. I'm never too sure about how much of what I say she understands. I look inside her nappy with relief. At least she had something to eat today. Or is it yesterday's dinner?

The pressure on my bladder becomes so strong that I have to release it that second. I look around the room: it's full of changing tables but not a single toilet. I reach out for a pile of Maja's nappies and place one of them next to the changing matt. I open it, lay it on the floor, and squat above it. Maja's face lightens up. I'm amazed that at twelve months she gets the joke. This nappy is unbelievably absorbent.

"Maja cried all day long," says Sarah when I meet her at the corridor. She pauses and scratches her head. I catch a glimpse of unshaven armpit.

"Does she get enough TLC at home?" she finally asks.

"Yes, and I still breastfeed her," I say.

"At twelve months? She does not need it."

The doorbell rings and seven other mothers walk in. The place is suddenly too crowded. I turn around and walk towards the doors. Maja and I get into our Ford Fiesta.

We pull out.

I want to go home-home. See my mama. Maybe we should drive there tonight? To Dover and then over the Channel… Have I brought enough nappies with me to last us for thirty-six hours? I thought once I had a family it would all get easier. But having my own family makes me miss everyone back home even more. Maja falls asleep and my eyes become watery. I turn on the windscreen wipers as if it is raining.

She wakes up when I stop the car. As soon as we enter the house, I run a bubble bath. I undress and get into the bath, too. The dimples on her cheeks become deeper, like my mama's, when she smiles; she starts splashing the water around her and I join her.

I always wanted to give birth to Maja in a bath. Instead, I was induced, tied to a bed. Pushing hard to a deadline. And then, peek-a-boo, she was out. My first thought after was: I don't ever want my daughter to suffer the pain of giving birth.

"*Kaczka*," says Maja pointing at the duck floating on top of the largest bubble.

I look at her and can't quite believe my ears. Her first word! She did not learn that from Sarah-three-fannies. Or anybody else, but from me, her mummy.

The tiles in the bathroom are now brighter orange. The duck is more yellow than a minute ago. I close my eyes and sniff Maja's head, inhaling the smell of her lemony down.

The following morning, it is too sunny to be driving. We leave the Fiesta in the garage and walk instead.

We pass a pigeon on the road, flattened by a car.

"*Kaczka*," says Maja.

She leans out of her pram, points at a yellow flower, a dog, a cat, and later a squirrel. They all have the same name: a duck. In fact, everything is a *kaczka*.

"I've got some good news for you," says Sarah when we enter the room where Maja will spend her day, like a prisoner.

"We have a Polish nurse starting today. If you want, he can speak Polish to Maja."

"A man?"

"Yes, from Kraków, like you."

I'm not from fucking Kraków. The doors open. It's Bohdan, my ex-boyfriend. He smiles. Maja returns his smile.

My stomach doesn't like surprises. It now feels like a heavily overloaded washing machine drum. My knees bend. I re-adjust Maja's shoelaces.

I can't possibly leave Maja with him. He must be well over forty now but he doesn't look it.

"You? In London? A nurse?" I ask in Polish, rising from the floor.

"I met this English girl. I'm taking a year off to be with her. I could not find a job as a dentist in London but they said that, in the meantime, I could be a nurse."

I jam my arms by my sides to hide my armpits even though I shaved them last night. Maja wants to join in the conversation.

"*Kaczka*," she points at me and laughs.

"I'm not a *kaczka*, I'm your mama," I say.

Bohdan laughs. Sarah giggles, too, even though—I'm pretty damn sure—she doesn't know what the hell is going on. A little boy playing with a toy tractor joins in. Then another toddler in yellow overalls. Soon the whole room is laughing. I'm the only one who isn't. I look at my watch. I'm running late. I excuse myself and go to the toilet. I give my husband a ring.

"Erik? It's me," I say. "Maja's new babysitter. I know him. I used to go out with him. I know his sexual fantasies... He is a bit twisted."

"In what way?" asks Erik. I tell him about the armpits. I can hear him smile. I smile back and I'm sure that he can hear it, too.

"Don't worry, love, he is not there alone with her. And you can watch them on Skype. Invite him over for dinner at the weekend," he says and I feel better.

I give Maja a hug. I kiss her fragrant head good-bye. When I reach the door, I stop to look back. She is climbing into Bohdan's lap and doesn't even register that mama is leaving her.

On the train I catch a glimpse of myself in the window. My face looks pale and I must have forgotten to brush my hair this morning. I find an old lipstick at the bottom of my bag and some mascara in the left pocket of my coat.

I put some lipstick on. A woman smelling of lavender lifts up her head from behind *Metro*. She looks at my lips. Her eyes say: "goes well with your coat." I want to hug her.

I bump into Adam, the IT guy, in the elevator.

"I found a spare laptop for you. It will work better with Skype." He winks at me twice. He looks even more cross-eyed than the day before.

The computer is a bit old and slow but I manage to sign in.

Maja and Bohdan are playing peek-a-boo. He covers his eyes and then opens them and says "Boo." Except, he is doing it head-down, looking at her from between his legs, hiding his head behind his muscular Kraków thighs—lifting one of them up whenever he says "boo", like he is operating some kind of heavy piece of machinery. I think of Erik when he jumps around playing with Maja, effortlessly, like a grasshopper dancing with a bee. Bohdan's face is red from being upside down, and from trying too hard. It's the first time it occurs to me how odd it must feel for him; no longer in total control—fixing teeth, making his patients sit still for hours. I almost feel sorry for him.

What really drove him to leave a good job back home; to come to London and make no money—working as a nurse?

A woman. What kind of woman, I wonder.

Maja gets bored with this game quickly. She approaches him and starts pulling his curls. She then gets a coloured pencil and sticks it into his left ear. At first it almost feels good to be watching her hurt him a little. All this time he does not react, as though he is now her patient, sitting on a dentist chair and waiting for his tooth to be pulled. I can't decide if he is doing it because he is kind or because he is so helpless. Maybe he doesn't know himself. His stillness is now so irritating that I can't watch it any more. I log out.

When I pick her up from the nursery after work, she is not in her usual "Pandas" room.

I take the stairs down and find her in the back garden. She is sitting in a little red car, being pushed around by Bohdan. She waves to me with her right hand, while her left hand is still on the wheel, steering. She looks surprisingly grown up. He looks knackered.

"How was her day?"

"Great. Had a fabulous day. A lot of kids were off sick today so we spent a lot of time together."

I take her out of the car and give her a hug. She is wearing a sticker on her chest, like a medal. It says: "I ate all my dinner."

"Would you like to come over to dinner at ours?" I ask him.

"Would love to."

"Saturday at six o'clock?"

"Yeah, I'm free then."

"Would you like to bring your girlfriend?"

Maja starts wriggling. She points at the doors making short, loud sounds: "OR!—OR!—OR!"

At five o'clock on Saturday Bohdan sends me a text message saying that his girlfriend, Polly, can't make it. Too late, I've already cooked for the four of us. When he arrives, it feels a bit surreal to have him in our house. As I take his coat, I'm trying to remember what loving him felt like.

"Nice parquet floors," he says. "My house in Kraków is a bit like that only bigger."

"Is it worth a lot less than houses in London?" Erik asks.

"I wouldn't be so sure any more. With the pound going down and the value of złoty rising…"

"Is that why so many Polish people are going back home now?"

"It's not just that. Most Polish men prefer to settle down with Polish girls. And vice versa."

Bohdan is wearing tight black leather trousers that make a funny noise when he sits back in his chair, like a quiet fart. Whether or not it was wind or Bohdan's trousers making a noise, Erik looks amused.

"Are you always so generous with your Baltic wind?" Erik asks Bohdan.

"It's my trousers," says Bohdan. "But I can fart. Freely. Something to do with my diet of cabbage," he says.

"The English are silent but deadly," says Erik.

"So when you fart, where do you do it? Alone, in the bathroom, like a wank, or silently, for example on a train full of commuters?" asks Bohdan, laughing. They don't say anything to each other for a good thirty seconds.

"And do you fart before, during, or after intercourse?" says Erik.

Bohdan stops laughing. I suddenly feel the urge to leave the house and look at them through a window. Maybe Bohdan would push Erik and—if I wasn't watching—Erik would hit him across his face. Would it make me forget about myself, about motherhood with its million little acts of violence a day, none of them significant, or even noticeable, like a ladder in a stocking or a broken fingernail? And then, when they stopped, would there be a moment of silence?

Bohdan's mobile rings. He spends ten minutes on the phone to Janka, his sister in Poland, a filmmaker, who just got European Union funding to make a new project.

Erik eats two bowls of soup and nothing else. Bohdan devours three bowls of barszcz and then eleven dumplings. All this time we talk about either our Maja or Bohdan's sister—and how clever they are. It feels like Janka and Maja should be related. Forty minutes later, Bohdan says that it's time for him to make a move.

"Thanks. It was great to meet you, finally," he says to Erik and shakes his hand.

"*Ciao*," he says to me and kisses me three times: left cheek, right cheek, left cheek.

That night Erik and I don't clear the table but go straight to bed.

Except, we don't quite get there. We put the empty washing machine on, and by the time it's spinning, I can feel its white metal doors open wide below me, the soapy warm water spilling everywhere, like warm waves of milk, coming in and out, again and again and again.

When the rinse cycle finishes, I turn around and see Maja's teddy on the kitchen counter. It gives me a dirty, cross-eyed look.

My left breast starts filling up.

Last Steps

The letter on the table was from the Sunrise Care Home.

Dear Miss Karen Smith,

We wish to inform you that your grandmother—Eva Schnitzel—has become very withdrawn lately. She has been watching late-night boxing matches on Sky Sports, and talking to the boxers. Sometimes the boxers talk back, she tells us. We are concerned about her mental well-being. Is dementia common in your family?

Yours truly,
Emma Brough, Senior Nurse

Karen slipped on her flowery summer dress. She put on red Chanel, and caught a fast train to Wimbledon. Running up the marble steps of the Sunrise Care Home, Karen smelled fresh lilies. Two more flights of stairs and she reached the doorway of Eva's apartment. The door made a wet squeak. Eva sat regally in her golden armchair, watching a boxing match on TV—with her fists clenched.

"Swartz-ma-cher," she chanted.

There was a huge golden vase of white lilies on the round oak table. When Karen touched the petals, the lilies stained her fingers with bright red dust.

"Ouch," she said.

On TV, Felix Brauer attacked Kurt Swartzmacher with a series of quick punches. Eva shouted, "Come on, Kurt!"

Karen noticed a new mobile table, parked by Eva's dimly lit bedroom. For reading in bed, she thought. Or for eating in bed. But why by the door? Maybe Eva used it like a Zimmer frame, or a walking stick?

On TV, Swartzmacher floored Brauer with a right hook. Eva unclenched her hands from the armrests. She counted along with the referee.

"One, two, three!"

At the count of nine, Brauer got up. His chest shone with sweat. His left eye was cut. Then one angry punch, up Brauer's nose. And then another, even more fierce, as if the fight was about a woman, and the golden medal didn't matter for him at all. Swartzmacher could kill—easily—thought Karen. Eva always supported the best, the strongest. The ones who needed no support. The obvious winners.

"Finish him," said Eva. Swartzmacher nodded his head—in agreement. Eva's fists closed again.

"Good match?" Karen asked. She was now standing next to Eva. They embraced; Eva's fists felt like two sharp diamonds pressed against Karen's back.

"Excellent match! Glad you came, my dear."

Karen sat on the edge of a chair beside Eva's throne. She took out *The Complete History of World War II* from her bag.

"Don't read—watch. Boxing gives you energy—like chocolate."

Karen put her book away. She stroked Eva's wise old hands, wrinkled like a forehead, with her elegant fingernails, each like the petal of a miniature lily. Eva spent a hundred pounds a month on her manicures. And who knows how much on lilies! She often said that it was her perfectly shaped nails that keep her brain so sharp. But the lilies? Why so many?

Eva sat forwards in her armchair. On the TV, Swartzmacher was now on the bench, with his legs wide apart, taking a break. He spat blood.

"I *love* you," said Granny.

Karen heard it a lot. You are so beautiful. You are so great. I love you. I'll never stop loving you.

"I love you too, Eva. But can we watch something more relaxing?"

"Boxing *is* relaxing, my dear. That's what soldiers do, between battles. Between wars."

This was the first time Eva had mentioned the war to her.

"Did you know many soldiers, Eva—during the war? Did you talk to them?" Karen often read about the war. She subscribed to *BBC History* magazine.

Eva didn't respond. She was watching the match again.

Felix Brauer's face dripped with blood. Swartzmacher's punches were longer, effortless, as if he was throwing a ball. This was clearly what interested Eva: will he kill, or not kill?

The referee then grabbed Swartzmacher by his arms, as if to say: "Not so hard. You are the winner already. No point in hurting him more then you need to."

Suddenly, Karen wanted to look at something else. The new table maybe.

"Is the table new? Can I see?"

"Move out of the way, Karen, let me see the result."

"You never tell me anything, Eva."

"I tell you everything, my dear. I tell you that I *love you*. I tell you that you are my *favourite* grandchild."

"But you never talk about the past. You never tell me about your Berlin days."

"When I think back, I just see you—instead of me."

On TV, Brauer fainted, with his eyes closed. Face first, his fists still in the air. The room filled with the warm orange light of an Audi advert. A black car whizzed through the Sahara, reached an oasis with palm trees, lions, and giraffes.

When Karen came to see Eva the following Sunday, the TV was switched off. Eva was staring at the black screen, holding a photograph. Karen could smell fresh lilies in the room again.

"How are you, Eva? Why is it so dark in here? Why are you not watching TV?"

"Come here, I want to show you something. This is a picture of me—in Berlin. In April forty-five, when the entire city was at a standstill—in the middle of the siege. You've seen it before, haven't you?"

Karen had a copy at home, framed by her bed. Eva—in the city which hadn't surrendered yet, jumping from one pile of rubble to another. She was wearing a rose-print skirt and a pair of stockings, with an elegant seam at the back.

"My legs survived. But my stockings did not. They laddered against a sharp stone. The run was too deep to be fixed."

"Did it cross your mind to take your stockings off and bury them?" Karen asked.

"No. The wind took care of them, blowing the stockings over the Unter den Linden, like a kite."

"Who took the picture?"

"My father. Later that day, he brought our 33mm Contax back home, developed the film, and then exchanged the camera for five loaves of bread." Eva paused and it was so quiet in the room that Karen could almost hear the lilies sipping water in the vase on the table. Maybe Eva thought that boxers looked pretty—like lilies.

"I got cross with father about the camera because I liked being photographed," Eva said. "I went to get the camera back. Walking down Unter den Linden, I got stopped—by two officers. One short and weak, with a babyish face. The other—strong, like Gulliver. With round glasses—for reading. I never trusted men who liked to read."

"Were they German?"

26

"No. Their uniforms were very dirty but fitted them well. They looked hungry and never said a word."

"Were they sad?"

"No, they laughed. They saw my stockings, flying in the air. They pointed at the damaged spire of the old church above them. It was called Gedächtniskirche. But I don't think that they could say it. It's a difficult word."

"Did they say anything at all?"

"No, they took out their guns and pointed them at my flowery skirt. It occurred to me then that I had little choice, but some choice nonetheless. The weak man would hurt me less, I thought. So I kissed him on the cheek. I had no time to think. Before I knew it, they put their guns away. They rolled up their sleeves."

Eva's chest went up. Her wrinkly cleavage had the perfect shape of a heart. It seemed like a very long breath.

"People who read are sentimental. Sentimentality often spells cruelty, Karen. Remember never to read—too much. Your mother liked to read."

"But what happened next, Eva?"

"I just stood there watching them. Transfixed. Bare-knuckled, the bookish man punched the weaker man. Three times. That was enough. He seemed to want me more, I think. Then, he came at me."

Karen thought about Eva's torn stockings again; the last surviving pair. She imagined the stockings on the very top of the Reichstag, fluttering like a flag.

"Did you escape then, Eva? Did you run away?"

"Turn the TV on, Karen, will you? It's time for the fights."

"But what happened?"

"He tried to kiss me but I slapped his face. After I slapped him, he fell on his knees, as if somebody shot him in the head. He began to cry, like a little boy who didn't get his prize. I stood over him."

"Were you scared?"

"No. He first touched, and then he kissed my bare knees."

"Did you want to be kissed?"

"It felt like I was the prize which he deserved. It felt like the end of the war. It felt like I chose him long before the fight, before the war. I then met him every night, in the ruins. He brought me books. And magazines."

"Was he British? American?"

"No. He lived in Berlin—after the war."

"The lilies, Eva. Do you buy them or—"

"They get sent—from Berlin."

"And who sends them?"

"A man."

"The man from the ruins?"

"Next week, he is coming, Karen. Moving in, next door. With all his books, I imagine. Vladimir's wife—aged eighty-five—has just died."

"And—is he nice, Eva? Tell me. Is Vladimir nice?"

"As nice as you, my dear. Bring me the table, will you?"

Eva's legs wobbled as she stood up from her throne, holding against the table. The wheels squealed on the parquet floor. Eva pushed the table until she reached her bed.

Karen's hand was shaky too when—back home—she replied:

Dear Emma Brough,

Thank you for your letter. Dementia does not run in our family. Women age, but from the feet up. Kind of.

Sincerely yours,
Karen Smith

Hello Poland

On the way up the escalator, a Warsaw escalator, breathing Warsaw air, Jan sees women's buttocks. Women's cheekbones, too. Always the same, here. They were exactly the same one hundred and sixty-four years ago, when he first kissed a woman's cheek, in Warsaw; when he first touched a woman's bare buttock, in Warsaw. And the many other Warsaw cheeks that he had kissed. How many? He can't remember now how many. Many. Like all these women, going up and down the escalator now. How many are there? The entire Warsaw? And are they really going up the escalator or just user-testing it? He looks for his daughter among the women. He wants to see her, he wants to find her, now. But there are only women here, just women. He imagines women as girls. Each woman as a girl in a pink coat. A girl called Poland. Like the country. A lost country; his lost girl.

A petite woman flies by on her beautiful blue wings, almost knocking Jan over. She does a quick whirl in the air, above the escalator, like a little air show, just for Jan. Jan looks at her buttocks and imagines what her cheekbones must look like. Round and full cheekbones like her buttocks, surely.

She lands right next to him, at the top of the escalator. "Maybe you could screw me in your mother's bed," she tells Jan, whispering in his ear.

Her face is round, with dimples, like his mother's but younger, of course. What did she say again? In Mother's bed? And screw? Mother would have been exactly two hundred years old now, if she were still alive. But she died last year.

Jan hasn't heard anyone talk dirty like that for years, he realises, after a good while. Together, they step away from the escalator. Is this part of a user-experience test, or is this for real? For almost a hundred years he has only heard Parisian obscenities, which were nice but stiff, like a school lesson. He wishes he could hear these words again. He wishes he could stay on the escalator. Stay with this woman, always. Stay in Warsaw. Test Warsaw, every day. Test this woman. And then re-test.

He goes through passport control for the semi-elderly. The woman can't join him of course. She is too young for a passport.

"I read in the paper that you were coming tomorrow," says the officer.

"A little present for the press, I'm here already," says Jan. He is surprised that the press still bothers to announce his arrival. A hundred years ago a vase of red roses had landed on a journalist's head. What question had made Jan so angry? He can't remember now.

"Is it for good? Can I have your autograph, for my wife?" the officer asks.

"Sure, but don't leave me alone with her. You know I only go for the married ones," says Jan.

The officer hands him a piece of paper that looks like an official document. He flips it to the other side and Jan signs it: "From Jan. I'm back. You have a lovely husband."

The officer takes the paper, looks at it. "You are a funny guy," he says. "Can you sign it again, please? The first signature was just a user-test of the paper, and the pen. I can see now that it works fine," he says. His nails are painted bright red. That's what young men do now with their nails.

Jan signs again. For real, now.

At the luggage reclaim carousel, he spots the woman from the escalator, his blue butterfly. The luggage is taking ages. Fucking ages.

"They haven't user-tested this properly," she tells him. "This shouldn't be taking so long."

He goes to a toilet and looks in the mirror. Is one hundred and eighty too old for an affair? He doesn't look a day over ninety, really. And still a villain. Women always fall for actors playing baddies, no?

He is back now, and the suitcases are coming, slowly, but they are coming. Her suitcase weighs nothing. A feather.

"Here," he says.

"Thank you." It sounds like an acknowledgement: You just touched my suitcase. This is fine, absolutely fine.

He was asleep for most of this delayed flight, and still feels a little sleepy. It would have made no difference to him if he were two hours late, or ten. Were they held up at the airport? Which city, which airport? The flight from Paris only takes five minutes, so what had taken them so long? Of course they no longer have countries now, just regions. To him it still feels like crossing the border, if you are a declared elderly person, with special borders built just for you, just like he remembers, from his young adulthood, there to make him feel safe; borders like a fucking walking stick; borders like a guide dog, which helps of course, with this anxiety of travelling. Otherwise older people, like him, feel less safe; they feel lost maybe, according to user tests.

A loud announcement is made to confirm the delay and a free taxi is offered in compensation, which is nice, really. He would get a free taxi anyway but to think everyone can get a free taxi tonight is so nice, he thinks again, so very nice. And easy. He likes this new niceness; positive user experiences. The taxis are inside the airport. They are inside the hall, landing right in the middle, which is convenient really, with the snow; this wet snow outside, which he doesn't have to experience. He will just look at it from his taxi, which will be fine, of course. Someone has user-tested it, so it must work.

A man in a green uniform puts all passengers heading towards the centre in one queue, their queue now. It takes longer to queue than to fly, always. Jan and the butterfly are the last ones. She smells nice, like lemons, limes, and melons.

Ah, melons! Lemons! Limes!

He could just inhale and inhale. Test and test. Jan simply smiles pleasantly—he thinks he can still smile pleasantly if he really tries; he is an actor after all, isn't he? Everything he does is a test, a game, an imitation of life. The man in the green uniform opens the doors of the taxi for them.

"Forum Hotel," he tells the taxi driver.

"It's now Hotel Forum," says the driver.

"Perfect, I'm staying in a hotel opposite, called the Indigo Hotel," she says.

"It's now called Hotel Indigo," the taxi driver corrects her.

Soon they're flying above the city, for just thirty seconds; so fast. So easy.

A hundred years ago the way from the airport was a narrow road. It's now an air highway. His favourite café in Ochota district has grown into a shopping centre with dozens of cafés; maybe hundreds, it seems, from above. The roads from above are cleaner than a hundred years ago but polluted with billboards advertising cheap flights to London for 10 złoty return, on borrowed wings, and Real supermarket's "barbeque in one-second" deals. He sees a group of teenagers milling around the mall. He's surprised that Polish teenagers look exactly like French ones. They look responsible: with jobs, books, things to do, user tests to take, assess, and write reports on. They are all informers. Informing and living. Living and informing.

Although they are not Polish, or French any more. They are citizens of User Experience, with the regional flavour: Warszawski, for example. Warszawski User Experience. Not French.

"I'm Hanka," the woman says. Her hand is so small, and smooth and pleasant to touch. He shakes it with both of his hands.

The taxi goes through the city centre and lands by Indigo Hotel, or Hotel Indigo, opposite to the Forum Hotel, or Hotel

Forum. Easy! A hundred years ago, the latter was one of the tallest buildings in the city. But now it seems dwarfed by the skyscrapers growing around it, above it, and underneath, deep in the ground.

Hanka gets out first. Buttocks. Ah, buttocks. He must stop looking. It's wrong to look. His daughter must be the same age, after all. He closes his eyes and just inhales the smell of her.

Melons! Lemons! Limes!

"Have a good evening," she says. Then she just hops away on her wings, half-flying, half-walking. The porter opens the doors for him. Is he that old?

At the hotel, when Jan asks about his hotel booking, the booking he took for granted of course—he booked like a thousand years ago, it seems—he is told that it's been cancelled.

"Really? Have you got any other rooms available?" he asks.

"We apologise. Tonight is so busy. No more rooms. We have a team of boxers staying here. But I can call Hotel Indigo for you if you like."

"Yes, please," he says. Do you know who I am, he wants to ask but not really. No, it's nice when people don't remember him.

"Are you following me?" Hanka asks. She's in the bar of Hotel Indigo, sitting on her own. She's got super legs, and her maroon dress with little red flowers couldn't be much shorter. Of course, she must have user-tested it, so it's not too short and not too long. It's perfect. She no longer reminds him of a butterfly. Now it's a fox. Her wings are put away.

"Yes, I decided to stay here instead, hoping to have a drink with you," he says. "Would you like a drink? Would that be easy?"

She selects a bottle of Gato Negro, a Chilean wine. Or really, wine from the city of Valdivia.

"You are much nicer in real-life than on MP9," she says. "You don't seem as tough. You are easy to talk to."

"Hmm, so you've seen me on MP9?" He takes off his glasses and wipes them with a tissue.

"Yes, and more recently on DVX."

She sips the first two glasses of wine very slowly, as if it were water. He needs to get back to eating and drinking more slowly, reacting more smoothly, the Warsaw way. She soon excuses herself "to make an important telephone call."

He looks around the bar. He could be anywhere, really: Paris, London, Copenhagen. A group of London men opposite him are getting drunk: quick shots of cranberry vodka every few minutes but their ties still remain intact. Jan loosens his soft cotton tie. It's so soft it feels like cotton wool. A hundred years ago, most foreigners he bumped into in Warsaw hotels were loud Russians. To avoid them, he drank in his hotel room rather than in the bar, where he could get drunk in his own bed, wearing his pyjamas. There are no Russians now, or Americans. Funny, he almost misses them. The world is cities, towns, villages. Must be a nightmare for children to study and remember!

After twenty minutes, as he is beginning to think about heading back to his room, Hanka reappears. And limes! And lemons! Melons? He can't smell melons now. A man in dark glasses with heavy frames passes them. He resembles the young General Jaruzelski. He has the same stiff-neck look about him.

"Are those glasses back in fashion?" she asks.

His fingers feel damp when he picks up his drink. He doesn't do politics but it's good to be speaking Polish again. Or rather, the Warszawski variety of Polish.

"I saw a picture of young Jaruzelski in a Parisian paper the other day. He wasn't wearing his glasses. He had the most amazing brown eyes, with long eyelashes," he tells her.

"Where were you when he declared martial law?" she asks.

"I was visiting a friend and had to stay when it was declared. It was nice to talk to her for longer. We ended up having lots of sex that night. We had sex, and cried and cried. Sex imposed by a curfew. And tears too. How old were you in 1981?" he asks.

"I was conceived then," she says. "I'm a by-product of a curfew."

"A beautiful by-product," he says. So she is young. Not even seventy yet. Like his daughter.

God, this feeling again, of panic, of anger, in his stomach and then deeper than the stomach, the black hole inside his stomach. The endless universe of his stomach which can't get tense, it just can't, because his stomach is not an organ anymore, it's just this vast emptiness, with his daughter inside, like he's devoured her over the past decades, with his endless worry about her, her absence, or her undefined presence, somewhere. His daughter is now this little stone, it seems, rotating in his stomach, around the orbit of the stomach's lining. He always feels her.

The smell of melons is suddenly back, and upsetting; too sweet. It's the sweetness he doesn't want to smell; too sweet to be around.

"Was martial law tested on the users, before it was declared? You know, the way we now test wars, before we declare them, with artificial intelligence, specially developed personas as enemies?" she asks, unaware perhaps of his sudden mood changing to a lower mood. He can hide moods, of course. He can hide tears, and anger, and panic too, even black holes in his stomach.

"No," he says. "User experience didn't exist then, you know."

"Sounds insane, that world. Unsafe. So what if martial law hadn't been declared?" she asks.

"You wouldn't be here?"

"Is it all so black and white to you?" she asks.

"Well, you know, of course it is. Jaruzelski found the golden formula. The solution to all evil. Martial law, and then Round Table Talks, which Americans—then Americans—replicated after democracy failed but with guns against people's heads so that people just talked, and didn't leave the table until they all filled in their feedback questionnaires. Then came the User Experience, which replaced all systems, even general elections."

"So when you worked for the secret police, was that white or black?" she asks, as if she hadn't heard what he had just said to her; hadn't registered any of it. Does she even know who Jaruzelski was? Jesus. He is suddenly worried about her too, as if she was his daughter. Was Hanka tortured? Refused contraception when democracy failed? Was she ever forced to give birth to deformed babies, like so many Polish women, in Poland, then? Can she not talk history, stories; can she only analyse user tests?

"I don't care about history. I care about you and what you feel right now," she says. "Are you experiencing any points of pain?"

Maybe she just wants to know about him, and why he is here. She wants things black and white, he thinks. User-tested. Simple.

No past, just easy presence. Like all of them now. Easy is the new successful.

"Well, I lost my daughter around the same time. She was kidnapped at a border crossing. We were going to Germany. They destroyed me, you know. To put it simply. They destroyed my life."

"And what, they also *destroyed* your career? Did you have to *flee* Warsaw? But what about her? Tell me about her," she asks.

"Poland," he tells her. "She was called Poland."

Her eyes widen. She takes a deep breath. Why a deep breath, now? She knows it all already, doesn't she? Everybody knows. People need enemies. They can't function without enemies. But she is not interested in enemies. It's strange, a little strange maybe. This lack of empathy in having enemies. She just wants to know about the daughter, her name. In isolation. An isolated problem. Poland.

"Actors are not very good informers. We can tell a joke but can't get any facts straight, can't read maps. We're a bit thick, really," he says.

She pours herself another glass of wine and orders another gin for him, without asking if he wants it. She is a clever woman, very clever, he thinks. Has she memorised his file, he wonders? Does she know everything about him? Has she user-tested his personality type?

"Still, I had a couple of meetings with them." He does want to give her a little background to Poland. "They put me down in their books as their informer. These books are now available for everyone to see. The papers love them."

"I'm surprised they haven't sentenced you already."

"Well, they wouldn't. The informers are now heroes, of course. So many informers were just early user-testers, really. Just doing it secretly, rather than openly. We were the early whistle-blowers."

The group of Londoners are now leaving their table. One of them picks up a half-full bottle of vodka. The tallest and youngest one looks at Hanka and gives her a big drunken smile. Hanka does not smile back. She must like older men after all; men over a hundred.

"At the airport. With your wings. Was that a set up? I mean, a user test?" he asks.

"Yes. It was the only way you would notice me," she says.

"Fair enough. Well done. You know what type I go for," he says, feeling more tired than a minute ago. "And you followed me all the way from Paris? And cancelled my booking at the Novotel?" He is almost laughing now. A tired laugh.

"I did. But don't flatter yourself. I only do that kind of thing for childhood heroes."

"What are you getting out of this?" He breaks open a pack of cigarettes. A cigarette feels good between his fingers. Like a new border. A shape. Something new to do. It could be a long night.

"I'll have one, too, please." These are healthy cigarettes of course, with vitamins and amino acids.

"Tell me who you are working for and I'll give you one."

She looks at him like it should be obvious, so obvious. "*Gazeta*," she says and she scratches her head. She has such lovely hair, in a bun; he wonders how long it really is. He wants to stroke her head, like her dad. Then he thinks of his daughter again. Poland. What a stupid name they chose, for a girl.

"Oh," and that's all he says. This is like little Poland sitting in front of him, he imagines, for sure it would be like that. He just knows it now. He feels it. He's sure of this. This is a perfect user test, except it is not.

"Your confession will sell very well," she says.

"Only if you sleep with me," he says, because he needs to know, confirm this quickly. And if she is, this is the only way to check. The only way to force her to tell the truth. Yes, or no? Black, or white? Sleep, or not?

"What, you are testing if I am your daughter, like for real?"

"Well, you wouldn't like to go to bed with your own dad, would you? *Jesus*. Even if you were really angry at him; not even in some sweet fucking revenge, no, just no. Not consciously. This is the best test, am I right? Do I remember well my informer's guidelines? A dad can do it to his daughter, surely, it happens sometimes, it happens a lot, but a daughter would never fuck him back, I don't think? Or initiate it?" He feels sick. What a sick test. What a sick conversation. And yet, this is it. User Experience. Life's become sexualised to the point of becoming fucking sexless. There are movies about men playing daddies and women playing their daughters. He's not in these movies—he would never—but he knows they're out there. Hundreds of them, with sequels. It's like sex is everywhere, so it might as well be nowhere, everything so ridiculously open, and endless, like his stomach, with this black hole he hates so much, just this pure uncontained anxiety, everywhere now, and all inside his body now, spilling out.

They are the only customers left. The barman looks bored as he inspects his cuticles. His nails are painted pink.

"How are things in Paris?" she asks.

"Not too bad. I still play villains: KGB agents and evil Moscow businessmen. I never play Polish guys. I mean, Warsaw guys. Kraków guys. The Parisians think maybe that we are not complex enough as characters. They think we are super boring. So well-organised. Always on time. Never drunk."

He asks for the bill and looks at his watch.

"Hanka, it was a pleasure to meet you. I'm very impressed with you and your interest in me. And maybe we should have sex sometime, if you are not my daughter. Or maybe we should user-test our personality types, if that is your wish, prior to fucking each other. But can I go now?"

"You are angry at me, aren't you?" She hands him a business card. "Promise you'll call. I can help."

"If I do, it'll be to discuss your naughty language," he says.

"At the airport?"

He stands and looks at her face again. Could she really write anything about him to make him a hero? The informer, the bad dad, who lost his daughter at a busy border crossing? Bad dad, but a good user-tester maybe, because he still feels something. And this would be a way to find his daughter. To become a tester, a tester with feelings. Just a tester of women. Women he loves. He still hopes to find Poland. That's all he wants. He wants to see Poland again. Just see her and say hello, and say hello again. Hello Poland. He doesn't want to know her story, her painful story, whatever happened to her when he left; when he let go of her hand; he doesn't want to analyse her points of pain, in every detail, like they now do with trauma patients. A point of pain is an opportunity in the user journey, of course. Pain is an opportunity. Opportunity for growth. For more user-testing. And then more, with more pain, and more opportunities defined, and more testing. And fuck that, he thinks. Fuck all that.

In his room, he takes a shower and goes straight to bed. Around four in the morning a gentle sound of rain wakes him. He opens the window but the sound seems to be coming from below rather than above. It's the team of boxers from the Novotel, drunk and confused it seems, or maybe they are just testing "drunkenness." They could be testing his reactions to drunkenness, or boxers. It's hard to say. They are walking in circles, maybe wondering which of the two hotels is theirs. He observes the streams of urine going in different directions on the marble pavement.

Maybe it's the feeling of emptiness and dull aggression that some call "reverse culture shock." It makes you do wild things, like pulling your hair out or crying for hours without any apparent reason. Like crying, urinating through the window is so liberating. It reminds him of the times in his childhood when he would take a shower and urinate under it. He hears a boxer swearing at him. He closes the window and writes Hanka a text message: "Meet me for lunch tomorrow."

He wakes up at midday. No time for breakfast. He tries to remember the dream he had. Grandma Stasia always said that you can only dream two kinds of dreams. "Little boys dream of glory and little girls dream of little things," she said. His was definitely a little girl's dream. It had something to do with feeding cats, planting cherry trees around a small house in the middle of a forest and then swimming in a lake, naked, and urinating while swimming. He runs his hand over the mattress. Not wet. Well done, he thinks.

Downstairs smells different, like a different hotel, with more fresh air.

"Mr. Kaleciński?" asks the receptionist when he walks by. "I've got a message for you." She hands him an envelope. It smells of lemons, melons, and limes. It's just a little note, tiny in his big hands. It says: "I'll bring your daughter to lunch so that you can say hello."

He puts the letter back in the envelope and closes his eyes. An hour left, he thinks, and then he can say hello. A hello.

In the lift now, going to his room, so that he can refresh and look nice, for his daughter, he closes his eyes and imagines Poland, his Poland now, in a restaurant, in exactly one hour from now. Hanka will introduce them, and then she'll go.

Goodbye, Hanka, he'll say. See you later.

Hello, Poland.

Poland will nod at first. Just nod. She'll look like little Poland, only now a mature woman surely, and beautiful, with red lipstick on her lips, and perfect eyelashes, and a nice haircut, a nice dress, maybe green. Hello, she will say back. Hello, Dad.

They will order something nice, something little. A risotto maybe, or pasta, like when she was a little girl, and they always had pasta or risotto together. He will ask: Would you like some wine? Red or white? And she'll say red or white, whichever she'll like, of course. It doesn't matter. A nice wine. She'll choose a nice wine.

Hello, he'll say to her after dinner. And after dessert: Hello.

Boyik

In the early twentieth century, Adam travelled to the United States on the ocean liner *Prinz Friedrich Wilhelm*. He took several trips, and each time, he returned to his village in eastern Poland. After his last trip, he built a large farmhouse for his wife Marta and "her" three children.

"Ours," she corrected him. "You are back home now. With us." They were in the garden, talking to their new neighbour, Anna.

"Is America nice?" asked Anna.

"Yes, but it's so good to be home," Adam said. "And it's Marta's birthday."

Marta looked at the sky; black clouds, on her birthday.

"I want to get you some daffodils," he said, and kissed her hand.

His beautiful slim figure in the garden now, by the stone stable. One raindrop, and then another—on her nose and then her forehead. A thunder so loud it sounded like a bomb exploding. A bolt of lightning. Adam fell to the ground as if shot.

"*Pomocy!*" he shouted. Marta shouted for help too, much louder. The children were shouting as well.

Neighbours came running. It started raining heavily, and the lightning struck again, twice, in the nearby forest. Marta took the children into the house. She heard more thunder. And then another. It felt hot inside, like a Russian sauna. Through the steamy windows, she saw more neighbours running towards Adam. They covered him with soil, as was customary, so that the evil spirits from the lightning got absorbed by the soil quickly. Adam was raising his hands; he was telling them something. Maybe he just wanted to be left alone? Was he praying? Marta wished she could hear his exact words. What was it that he needed, just then? Other than what was customary?

When the thunderstorm stopped, Marta ran out again, barefoot, the children following in her footsteps, barefoot too, stepping on her heels and toes. Adam wasn't moving, but his mouth was open, as if still gasping for air. She grabbed his half-buried hand. It felt warm, and then colder and colder.

"We must bury him immediately," said the priest, who was also one of the neighbours.

"Not in the cemetery, but in the forest. Near the house, please. I want him near us, please," she said.

The priest agreed. Marta asked the neighbours to help her carry the body to the forest. The entire village pitched in, working to bury him properly, in a coffin. The neighbours hugged her and told her how much they loved her. How they loved her children. How God was great, and he would look after them now.

After the funeral, Marta continued living on the farm, with her *boyiks*, as she called her three little cute boys. She never called them "three little cute boys" of course because she never had any patience for words, so she used a diminutive form of the word "boy" instead. The English word "boy" arrived from America, with one of Adam's happy returns, and stayed with them even after his death. She employed ten extra men to help on the farm. She paid them with gold brought from America. And with chickens.

Overnight, the cows were worth as much chickens, and chickens as much as carrots, and the Great Depression began. She bought seven more cows, very cheaply, and hid them in the nearby forest. She had a pen in the forest which she concealed with shrubbery.

The next day, a couple of border bandits invaded the farm asking for cows. Marta now had thirty cows hidden in the forest, not far from Adam's grave. In order to distract the bandits, she picked up a large cock, with her left hand, and a hen with her right, and began hitting one of the bandits with the cock and the hen, taking turns, until she killed both birds, and the bandits ran away.

The boyiks had chicken soup for three days, and for three days they didn't remember that their father was no longer around, or so Marta hoped. Every day she just hoped that she could distract the boyiks from his absence and give them something else instead, or at least deal with his absence in a way which would not harm them.

It was of course a scary prospect to be on her own, on a farm, with three boys, one of whom was a little girl called Barbara, who cried more than the boys, or just cried longer and louder, or never quite stopped crying. It often seemed that crying was Barbara's default setting; she cried more often than she did not. For this reason Marta hid the fact Barbara was a girl, because she thought the bandits would not mind a crying boy as much as a crying girl maybe. A crying boy could be ridiculed, while a crying girl would not be forgiven; she would be treated worse than a crying boy, surely. So she dressed her in boyik's trousers and shirts and never referred to any of the children by their names.

One day, one of them—the one she and Adam had called Romek—asked her, "When is daddy coming?"

She felt sadness, and rage, and panic, and then nothing at all, as if it didn't matter what she felt, really.

All three of them looked up now when she said: "Boyiks, I have something important to say. Daddy is gone. We buried him because he was dead."

"Did he leave you?" asked Romek.

"Daddy said he would be back in the evening," said Barbara, and then she started crying.

"Did he cheat on you?" asked Adam, who was the youngest and named after his father.

"Yes," she said. Because it was all true, what they said, simultaneously, all three, like a symphony. Life cheated her, because her husband used to always be back in the evening, if he wasn't away in America, but not today. And he did leave.

He left her for his new afterlife, with his new bride, death, or lightning.

Her boyiks stayed so calm. It troubled her how calm they were. Because weren't boys supposed to be trouble? Didn't boys need to make mischief?

"I want scrambled eggs, please," Romek finally said.

She had no eggs left in the house so she told the boyiks to hide under their beds, and went to visit the neighbours to borrow a couple of eggs. It was good to be outside and just walk, even if it was only five or six steps. It was still a walk.

The neighbour's farmhouse looked smaller than hers. Unlike her farmhouse, it wasn't built with American gold. It didn't resemble an American farmhouse. She had no idea what an American farmhouse might look like, but the house itself—the bricks, the doors, the silver roof—didn't have the feel of foreign wealth like hers; wealth of a better kind than if you had stayed in the village. This house was poorer. She entered it without knocking. It had no wooden floors like hers. The floor was earth. Of course, she thought now, it was lucky Adam travelled to America, when he was still alive, even if he had to cross many borders illegally, the Prussian border to start with, which was only just around the corner from her neighbour's house, next to a town called Raczki.

Through the window, she could see the roofs of the houses on the other side, past Raczki, in Prussia. They looked different, these roofs, built with different money, different kingdoms, and languages. They were red rather than silver.

The neighbour, Anna, always had eggs or whatever Marta asked her for. She just gave her anything, even if she had nothing left for herself, because Marta always bought things from them: cows, chickens, and recently more land, which was a better investment than cows, Marta thought. Anna was sitting on the floor, playing with her children. They had kittens. The children were all quiet, just like her children. Marta wondered if this was because they sensed fear, the border bandits, killings; the way rats somehow knew when to vacate Raczki prior to terrible storms.

"Other than eggs, would you like anything else?" Anna asked.

"Yes, can I have more land, please?" asked Marta.

A few days after the chicken soup was all eaten, and the couple of eggs eaten too, the border bandits went through Marta's new land, and she attacked them on their horses, hitting them with another cock and a hen, until both the cock and the hen died. On this occasion, too, the bandits quickly withdrew, and the children ate chicken soup for two weeks this time, as the cock was much larger.

After all the cocks and hens had been killed in her battles against the bandits, Marta was only left with a pig, thirty cows, and eggs borrowed from the neighbours. She felt not just hate, but rage, towards the bandits, some of whom were just regular border smugglers but they had guns, so she called them "bandits." Her biggest worry was that she couldn't hide her rage, because it was of course too ugly to hide. The ugliness spilt over. Her ugliness. She felt ugly. If only they told her that she could always stay, here, on the farm. If only they left her alone, because she had no husband. But no, they kept returning, until, one day, instead of fighting them, she just gave them one of her cows. Just like that, she said: "Here. A cow. Take the cow and don't come back. I have nothing else."

But this cow was clever and it returned. Like a dog. It came in the night and mooed and mooed outside the nearby stone stable, in the exact spot where Adam had been killed by lightning only a year before, between the tree and the chick house. And when it mooed and mooed, the neighbour's dog started barking, and then the dog in the next village, and then a few dogs in Raczki, and then in Prussia too, dogs barked. Marta imagined American dogs barking also, everywhere. She opened the doors and let the cow into the stable. She put her arms around the animal, as if it was her long-gone husband, and she cried and cried, and the cow continued mooing only a little now, humming little moos. Then the boyiks came to the stable and hugged the cow as if it was their father.

They had to hide the cow, because who would believe them that the cow was so clever it escaped the bandits and came back home? They would be accused of stealing the cow back, for sure.

But it was very late, so Marta left the cow in the stable and went back to bed. She thought of Adam. Oh, Adam, she thought. Then she slept, because she was tired. In the morning, she woke the children and took them to the forest with the cow. It was spring, and the garden was full of daffodils, and for a moment, holding hands with her boyiks, Marta felt happy, as if she had tricked the entire world. The cow, the children, and Marta, like a family now, reunited. Happy together again.

The forest had daisies, which came really early that year. They were daisies with pink petals, rather than white. Impure, blood-drinking daisies. And blood? There were no dead people in the forest, other than Adam's grave. He had a grave in the clearing. Marta thought of it as a kind of memorial to their happy marriage, with just a hump on the fresh spring ground and some new grass coming out like new baby hair, and a little white cross made of birch wood on top of the grave.

The boyiks hated coming here, especially Barbara, who cried, and they often kicked the grave and the cross and shouted at their father for leaving them, or they squatted on the grave and screamed into the ground, with their fingers making little holes, in despair and longing and the great desire to be heard and loved. It was hysterical but good, and Marta often told them, "I know how it feels." But these words never helped, and the children maybe wanted to hear something else. It troubled her she didn't know what it was that would help, to make them stop crying, especially Barbara. And whether it was important for her to stop, or quite the opposite. Maybe she needed to cry now, even if it scared the cow and the children. Emotions were scary, overwhelming for the children too, but even these feelings subsided, eventually. It was important not to lose sight of the fact that even if the grave was being kicked and abused, it was just a grave. Not her husband. Her husband, her dearest Adam, was dead but the children were alive, beside her, taking a little walk deeper into the forest. And God? God maybe too was a bandit that she needed to fight.

"Shall we go see the cows now?" she asked the boyiks, because the cows were only a few minutes away from where they were now, and she could almost hear the little snoring noises, as if they were little pigs. Little Adam said, "Mm-hmm," and then Romek said, "Yes, please." Only Barbara didn't answer.

"Barbara, where are you, my sweet girl," she shouted, forgetting she never used their names anymore, especially their full names, especially Barbara, or any of her many adorable diminutives: Basia, Baśka, Basieńka, Basiunia, Basieczka, Bańka, Baś, Barbusia.

She was frantic, worried. She ran through the forest back to the grave, pulling the other boyiks along, wondering if it would have been easier to lose a child or a husband. She hit a tree with an elbow, a beautiful birch tree, and then another tree with her knee, an old oak, but she kept on running. Adam's knee hit a tree too, a wild apple tree, so she placed him high on her shoulders, so they could move faster. It was then she realised that while she missed her husband of course, and missed him deeply, her life was so busy with the children. Maybe she loved the children more, not because they were alive, but because they were hers, and so little: her boyiks. Adam had never been fully hers; he had been his own person, he had travelled to America and back. She could live without him. She didn't need him. Not desperately. But she couldn't live without Barbara. Or Romek. Or little Adam. Never!

They reached the grave, and Barbara was there, crouching on top of the grave, shaking, in her boyik's trousers, all wet, smelling of shit. It was the sweetest smell, child shit, because it was just the smell and nothing else; nobody else here, with her girl. She embraced her as if she only just gave birth to her. Adam was still on her shoulders, pulling her hair like reins. Romek, like the father of the family now, age six, put his arms around his mother and his sister, and it felt good, so good. But did it feel good for him, or was it too much, too early, too much responsibility, too much to carry on his shoulders?

All Marta managed to say was: "I don't know what it must feel like for you, unless you tell me." And she didn't just mean to say it to one of them. She said it to all her boyiks. And it was only then that Barbara stopped crying.

Basic Wash

Mummy said: "I'll only be five minutes. I'll just wash the car, and be back."

I then often imagined her back with me and Daddy, with our Volvo all clean, and a few extra tokens from the Ready Wash— each with a picture of a car, ready to go in my wooden box, full of tokens from past washings.

Then one day I took out the box and said, "Can we take the Volvo to the Ready Wash, please?"

"We can, Sammy."

"And Mummy?"

"We have no Mummy—in the car. No Mummy."

Dad then drove slower than usual. He passed my nursery building, and then Granny's pink house.

The washing place was made of red bricks. It had a flat roof, like our garage but it was much larger. Big enough to fit a truck, or a digger. I opened my box and gave Dad my most polished token. It clinked as he put it in the slot. We drove in. Dad then said, "I love you."

"I love you, Daddy."

The Volvo was sprayed with bubbles. I licked them through the glass but only tasted my strawberry Hubba Bubba.

"How long, Dad?"

"Five minutes."

"How long is that?"

"As long as one episode of *Peppa Pig*."

Good, good. *Peppa Pig* always ended quickly, and so would this.

"Can I open the window, Dad? I want to smell the bubbles."

"OK, let's see what happens."

I felt cold minty water on my nose, and face. When I licked my mouth, it tasted like salty bath water, only bitter. More peppery.

"Close it, Dad! Close it now!"

A blue pine tree began rolling in front of the car, coming closer and closer, rolling quicker and quicker. Bang! Bang! Bang! It hit the car many times. Our car rocked. It got darker. I wanted to rock too.

"It's OK, son. These are brushes. And minty bubbles. Nothing to be scared of. They will go away in a minute. They won't get us now that the windows are closed."

"It's too dark and too loud in here."

Dad turned on the light above his mirror. It gave off a nice orangey light like in my parents' bedroom.

"Only four minutes to go, son. Can I turn the light off now?"

"No, I want to watch." I heard the brushes scrubbing the back of the car.

"I hope the battery won't die."

"What's a battery, Dad?"

"It's like a car's heart. When it stops working, the car dies."

"Will I die?"

"No, you'll never die. And neither will I. Everybody will—but we won't."

I knew about dying. People died when they stopped being pretty, or when they got sad. Sometimes they died young of something with a long name that made them scream.

"Where was I before I was born, Dad?"

"You were a little spider, crawling in our bath. A beautiful yellow spider, like a ray of sunshine. Different than any boy ever born. That's why we called you Ray. Your second name."

"And then?"

"I made you into a little boy."

"How did you make me, Dad?"

"Very carefully, with all the tools I could find."

"Was Mummy helping you, Dad?" Not all bubbles had been washed away. I could still see some on the windshield.

"Yes, she was there too. We made you together."

I looked up to see Daddy's face but only saw his chin. I took Daddy's face in my hands and moved his hairy face down, holding onto his beard as hard as I could.

This was better. I could now see his eyes and nose and mouth.

"It hurts, Sammy. You need to be gentle with faces."

"But how long?"

"Three minutes left."

"So please, tell me, Daddy. Tell me how you and Mummy made me."

"While watching the news on TV."

"But how?"

"I rubbed Mummy's feet. Then we kissed."

"Who kissed whom?"

"Mummy kissed me first, I think. Yes, I think it was her."

"Could you still watch TV and kiss?"

"I think we might have turned the TV off. Or maybe we put it on pause like when it's dinner time. Then I stroked her back."

Dad turned on the radio. I heard slow sad music. I thought of Snow White's mummy.

"Daddy?"

"Listen to this, Sammy. It's Bach. Bach is important. He was a great composer."

I scratched the side of Dad's seat with my longest fingernail, the one Daddy missed this week, when he cut my nails. Would Mummy miss it too?

I thought about kissing.

Perhaps mummies and daddies kissed on the sofa all night long, rubbing each other's backs and feet when they got tired of kissing. Maybe they sometimes had a longer break. They made a quick round of cheese on toast to keep them going, like when I came home from my nursery yesterday. And then they had a small drink of Tesco Pressed Cloudy, to help them kiss even longer.

I took the Hubba Bubba out of my mouth. I placed it under my seat, where I could feel wires and old paper cups. I tried to kiss the bubbles on my side window. But it didn't feel right. The bubbles stayed where they were, on the other side. The window looked steamy. My lips felt sore and cold. It wasn't very nice at all.

Dad's back was silent still; his fingers holding the wheel. The music was slow. Very slow.

"Dad, what comes after kissing?"

"Nothing—just more games."

"What games?"

"Tickling games. Pillow fights. Hide 'n' seek."

At nursery, a boy called Evangelos had told me about "dirty sex." He said that it was what all parents did, wearing nothing. They had to do it in order to have children.

"What is sex, Dad? Is it dirty?"

"Sex is what adults do when they run out of things to play with. When they no longer have things to talk about, son. It's just another activity. It's what you do after stroking the feet, and kissing. That's all. It's nothing, really. Nothing to be sacred of."

What if what came after kissing wasn't very nice. What if mummies turned into millions of little spiders? Not yellow but black, crawling through daddies' ears?

There were spiders at my nursery. They were called "false widow spiders" and they had come to England with bananas sent from countries far, far away. They closed my nursery for a day to get rid of the spiders. They could hurt children, they said.

What if banana spiders walked one by one, marching, until they reached Daddy's heart, spinning webs until his heart almost stopped. Maybe that's why Dad looked so scared sometimes.

"How did you *sex*, Daddy? Will you tell me?"

"With pleasure. Like a two-piece wooden puzzle, fitting well."

"How well?"

"Sometimes my share was just ten percent."

"What's ten percent, Dad?"

"Well, if you have a hundred car tokens in your pocket, and use only ten, that's ten percent gone."

Before the funeral, I took out my wooden box and slid a few tokens into Mummy's mouth, one by one, in case there were car washes there too, so that she would quickly wash the car, and be back. I'd counted ten then, maybe eleven tokens, in case she was given more cars than just one.

"How many more to have a hundred, Dad, if you already have ten?" Would a hundred small tokens fit in her small mouth? Would she need a hundred, or would there be no hundred cars there?

"Ninety, son."

"And how long did you do your puzzle, Dad? With Mummy?"

"It only took five minutes. Like a basic wash. See, we now have one minute left."

"Was it a stick puzzle, Dad?"

"We made all kinds of puzzles: stick puzzles but also construction puzzles, tiling puzzles, transport puzzles, disentanglement puzzles, lock puzzles, folding puzzles, combination puzzles, and mechanical puzzles, son. Always just two pieces, so it wouldn't take long at all. And how they fitted was different. Each time. Forty percent to sixty. Twenty to eighty. Ninety to ten. Ten to ninety. Fifty to fifty. Eight to ninety-two."

Daddy was not a *hundred* percent now, for sure. With my sleeve, I wiped Daddy's nose, and cheek and mouth. I took Daddy's hand off the wheel.

I first stroked and then kissed Daddy's hand—till the water fell away from his eyes.

Daddy took a different route back: past the park, and my favourite playground. When passing narrow streets, all cars waited for us to pass first, even larger families, in their larger cars.

We were different from them now. Not smaller. Not bigger. Just different.

Just us.

Belgian Passion

Before I met you, I didn't believe in suicide or love at first sight. No matter what happened during the day, I would come home, cut up a potato without peeling it, sauté it, and have it with mayonnaise, followed by a cigarette.

Then my wife, Marie, would come home. We liked to watch TV together, especially cooking programmes. Our favourite was Nigella Lawson. On Belgian TV, Nigella spoke in Flemish with French subtitles running below her bosom. Her lip movements didn't match the dubbed voice of another woman. Sometimes Nigella would stop talking but her Dutch voice would carry on. I used to find it hilarious. My wife didn't: "Why don't they let her speak English? We all know English in Belgium."

We would often order a takeaway of mussels, French fries, and strawberry beer. Then we used to shower, make love, have another shower, and then fall asleep, back-to-back, making sure that our buttocks were not touching. If we didn't make love, we would go to bed dirty. If I saw Marie having a shower before going to bed, it meant she expected me to have one, too.

We were Belgians, which meant we didn't really exist. Marie talked a lot. She was half French. I was only quarter French. "You are so Dutch," she used to say. I didn't think I was very Dutch or French. I didn't believe in nationality, flags, or borders. I didn't have any faith in languages and their separateness—they all grew from one another like potatoes, which could be cultivated in any soil.

I worked as a forester outside of Brussels. We had lovely forests in Belgium, not very big, though. I knew every tree. But not even in the middle of the forest would I feel alone with myself. There was always a light somewhere in the distance.

Once, a child got lost in my forest. I found him. I offered to carry him to the police station. He bit me on the leg.

I didn't want to have children. They scared me. I didn't know how to talk to them.

My wife's chest, too, fascinated me no more than camel's humps on a desert island or two balloons filled with water in an empty room. I didn't want to touch them too much in case they burst.

Marie asked me once if I fancied Nigella.

"Yes," I answered. But I wasn't so sure. She burst into tears. We never watched Nigella again.

That night, I didn't go home. I couldn't. I took the last drag on my cigarette and looked inside a pub called "Belgian Passion." I saw you ordering your chips.

Everyone I had shared a plate of chips with thus far, would devour them without any thought, but you were a slow eater. You put one chip between your fingers and stared at it. You smelled it. You made little indents in its flesh with your fingernails. You broke it up into two perfect halves. You arranged the rest of the chips on your plate into a perfect circle, like a child's drawing of the sun, full of rays. You looked at me through the window; you smiled; I walked in.

You reminded me of myself in a way I couldn't quite define: a flashier copy, maybe slimmer, or younger? Not even for a moment did I think about my wife, and whether or not she would try to fight you as if you were another woman, a Nigella of a different kind. I already knew how—back at your place—you would cut up a potato in thick slices, each slippery as a fish, its white flesh softened in the hot oil, pores opening up.

We sat together, watching each other eat, as the chips disappeared from the plate. When there was only one left, you reached for it and then hesitated. I picked it up and threw it behind us. It landed on a woman's face. She screamed.

"Silly tart," you whispered to my ear. You grabbed my hand and pulled me towards the door. It was only then that I noticed that we had the same haircut, the same baggy trousers and similar blue shirt with white stripes. It didn't matter if we were being chased or not.

A week later I moved out of Marie's flat. You suggested we go for a little trip to the Ardennes before deciding what to do next.

We stopped at a chippie. You asked them if you could prepare a portion of *pommes frites* for me. They let you into the kitchen. You cut up a potato into thin slices. The boy serving chips looked at you and smiled. He asked you for your number. You wrote the number on his forehead with a Montblanc pen. My heart clenched like a fist.

I had a gun in my bag; all foresters in Belgium did. We walked into a small valley that hid us from the rest of the world. The boy followed us. It was only then that you saw me crying, I think.

"Love me—love my boys," you said.

I took out the gun. It fired twice. You made a thud like a deer. I don't remember what the boy sounded like. I was ready to kill myself, too—please, believe me—but there were no more bullets left in my gun.

You stayed there, with the boy. I caught the last train to Brussels; I couldn't wait to get home.

I grow my own potatoes now in the middle of the forest, between the birch and the pond. It's the *binst* variety, from my region, the best in the world. Try frying them twice in beef dripping, once at 160 degrees, then again at about 175. They mustn't be cut too thin.

A Happy Nation

I don't believe this is an emergency for Great Britain, officer. It's just a crisis, you know, a little crisis. See, in an emergency, you call the ambulance. You call the police. But a political crisis is different. It's just an inconvenience.

So you can relax, really. Fully. Entirely. Relax. You can even fall sleep. The world won't see. And no, you haven't woken me up. Please, do come in. I was wide awake anyway. I just couldn't sleep. I had an awful nightmare which woke me up. I was expecting you, really.

How is it, this present crisis, officer? How is it for *you*? Empty streets, shops closing down, and all the immigrants gone away, as if on holiday; as if it was August. All of them but me. The only one now refusing to leave. Yes, I know, Polish immigrants were less than two percent of the population but it does feel a little empty without them. No? Not for you? Well, I guess I am still here. You *all* know me, Krystyna Kowalska.

You are doing your job. I understand. It's all right. You all seem so innocent, you, immigration officers. Like history never touched you. And please, do sit down. You don't have to stand up to interrogate me.

You are just too nice. You like me, don't you? That's the problem. You like me a lot.

But how are you feeling? Because, you know, I am *fine*. I am always *fine*. But *you*? Have you been unhappy these last few years, with me, just me, left? With this isolation? Have you tried calling anyone? Does it feel like you are always unhappy or only sometimes? Every holiday you now go to Wales. And if you were Welsh, well, you'd have nowhere to go. Are you quite happy now, where you are standing? I can't quite see you with this light in my eyes.

No, you are not upsetting me by asking me for my ID. Not at all. Although you ought to know who I am by now. I am used to having my ID checked. At home, in Poland, we all have IDs, many IDs. But I still love it here, with ID, or no ID, I feel loved, just loved by everyone: neighbours, colleagues, shopkeepers, and maybe that's why I've been refusing to leave. Because I am just a happy person, every day, even if I go through immigration checks, every day, or when I am searched on the street, or interrogated in the middle of the night, like now, I like it here. I am still happy, and there is nothing you can do to upset me. Not really. Because you are also so nice, so kind. But please, like always, let's talk first. Let's talk, before the interrogation starts. I like small talk. Do *you*?

Are you looking at this pink teddy? It makes me so happy! Christmas present from my father, when I was six. I lived in Gdańsk. Tanks encircled Poland then. I was lucky not to see them but I could feel them, like a rope on a throat. Or more like snow, which never stops snowing, and covers everyone and everything, until you can't breathe.

Yes, this is my father. Yes, that's right. He does resemble Lech Wałęsa. Wałęsa made me happy, too. He spoke to us like a fearless poet. We all believed him because he had faith. He was fearful only of his wife. It made me happy when he spoke, when he said, "Let's do it." And so history became a Nike advert from the future; a sport you played—like hockey—with your own history stick.

And yes, I still play with Barbies. I really do. I won this one in a rope-skipping competition. Nobody had Barbies in Poland then. Not very many people. It felt like I was the first. The first little girl with a Barbie. General Jaruzelski imposed martial law on me and my Barbie. But martial law made me happy because the tanks didn't come. Not many. They stopped. And it stopped snowing. And sometimes, because of the curfew, we would stay at friends' houses for sleepovers. Lots and lots of sleepovers. They made me happy. The growing solidarity in everybody's bedrooms. Baby-boom time. The Wałęsa and Jaruzelski time. Jaruzelski, our last communist leader. The benevolent dictator. The man behind the Round Table Talks, which made me happy because I saw political enemies sitting at one table, talking, discussing the future, arguing, exchanging different opinions, but never leaving the table, for three months. Perhaps we could have tried that here. Oh, happy times!

We still have time, don't we? You're not in a rush are you? So let me tell you what else made me happy. The Berlin Wall, oh yes, the Berlin Wall. Or rather, us jumping into little Fiats and driving all the way from northern Poland to Berlin, for over twenty hours; big families in their little Fiats, all driving just to see the Wall, the falling Wall. Soon after, Sebastian—who was half Russian and half Czech—asked me out to see *Gremlins 2*.

Then, a long kiss on the school bus with a German exchange student called Hans. Hans was not a great kisser—he just wasn't, officer—but even he made me happy. And I was scared to tell my grandmother. She was one hundred percent whitish, as I see it now. Three-quarter Polish and one-quarter something else, undetectable now of course.

Yes, *whitish*, you heard that right, officer. The White Other category, in other words. Before your time, perhaps? So let me explain.

Whitish used to be an ethnic group in the UK Census: it described people who, no, were not British, but who self-identified as white persons. This meant that the White Other group contained a diverse collection of people of non-British birth, religions, and languages.

Oh, are you sleepy officer? Are you looking at this picture? My grandmother. Beautiful, wasn't she? She had no British blood in her, not even a drop. She only spoke Polish, except for a few Russian swear words, which can have an influence on the purity of one's blood, as you know. Her great-grandfather came from Vienna, so she could also be a little Austrian, German, Slovenian, Romanian, Jewish, or even Italian. But she said she was happy, very happy that we had these exchanges in schools, so soon. That I could kiss a German.

"But who else, Krystyna?" she asked. "Who else do you want to date? How about a British man?"

"A British man, *Babcia*?" I wasn't so sure.

Yes, let's have a glass of wine. Thank you. Glad you found it in the fridge. Good idea. Before we start. I can warm up *pierogi* for us if you like? How would you define "British," officer? Do you know who you are? Did you learn about Great Britain in your history classes? The history of colonisation? Oh, you only learned about crop rotation and the Middle Ages, and then skipped to World War I?

Oh, I like the British. You all wear hats, like you, officer. And even if you don't wear one, it feels to us immigrants as if you did. You know, even in bed, you wear invisible hats which make you look so distinguished. A person in a hat must be right.

Why am I here, you ask? You want to start? Is this your first question? I'm sure I've told you before. Can I still sip my wine, please? I came to Great Britain to mix my blood. This was my only reason, which I gave to the border control guard. Not the benefits, not the work possibilities, I said to him, but sexual intercourses with a Brit.

"Just the one Brit?" he double-checked.

"Yeah," I answered. "One Brit. I met him in Poland, on another school exchange. He's British. But he is actually one-fifth Spanish. And a little Irish. Or just from Liverpool."

He yawned, just like you, just then, a minute ago, and he let me in.

What? You don't have that option on your form? You don't have sex? Sorry. Just tick "other reasons."

Later that year, Great Britain opened its borders to Polish people. And the enlargement happened just sort of *naturally*. With no protection, you might say now. Absolutely none.

Yes, these are my children. As babies. Fresh from the hospital. Nice pictures, aren't they?

From the delivery room at St. Thomas's Hospital, while pushing out my baby, everything seemed perfect, in every way. Childbearing made me very happy because I had a great view despite the great pain: the Houses of Parliament.

Ah, like a baby. You must be tired, officer. I'll just tell you a quick bedtime story now before you wake up. Isn't it funny that I look like you? You must be British. White British.

So what is the difference between us?

Don't you say that if you look like a duck, swim like a duck, and quack like a duck, then you are a duck? Even if you are not? I know, I know. You don't like our *delikatesy*. Not so much the sausages and the bread but more the design of the shop signs. The fonts we use. You hate Arial, all in caps, too, and red and white is just not a good colour combination, design-wise. I know, I know, you need a third colour for better branding, like the French, but we only have two. Yes, you can tell we don't study art and design in schools the way you do in Great Britain. And your signs are *great*. But how come you don't mind the Indian corner shops any more, or the Jamaican fruit and vegetable market on a Monday morning? Or Chinatown? Why *us*? Why *me*?

But I don't think it's all about appearances, really, our shade of white—eggshell or potato—only clear to you if we open our mouths. But what if we stay silent, or suddenly speak just like you? We could pass for indigenous Brits, couldn't we? After all, isn't the Queen a little German, and even a little Polish? And can you tell by the way she speaks?

I can speak English like a British person now. And that's exactly why you want me go, isn't it? Because you've lost control. You can no longer tell me from the others. White Others. I could be White Other, or I could just be white. The great white. You'll never know. I've assimilated in everything: education, sense of humour, style, and now also my speech. So I am a threat. Because what if I am actually a little *better* than you? Not much, just a *little*. A little cleverer. Funnier. Prettier. More organised. Not much. Just that tiny bit. Yes, it must feel like I am keeping you on your toes. I can't help it. It's just the way I am. But you need to develop too. You need to meet me halfway. I need to teach you manners maybe. My manners which are about telling the truth and facing the truth, in order to become greater than great. Which you don't see just yet, you don't see that process, and you perhaps never will; you can't. Besides, it's too late. I *am* leaving. Finally. Because I am a bit worried, just a little bit worried about the gun I see poorly hidden under your nice jacket. You've never brought a gun to my house before. I am just worried that when I stop talking to you, you will start talking to *me* more and more, and then I don't know what you will say. So I just want to remember you as a nice person who said nothing, nothing much. Someone nice who came here now and again, listened to me, and never caused me any harm.

Besides, the views from the train will be good, still good. I might stop in Normandy for a day, just for a little dip in the nice sea, or just for a modest beer somewhere in Germany, which is a nice country, too, with some nice designs of beer labels. Then, I will travel across Poland and then Ukraine. Then, deep into nice Russia, until it becomes nice China. I'll order a take-away and I'll sit by the embankment thinking of how it reminds me of London, that part of Shanghai, its design, and of all things great, which somehow got diluted by all this niceness, especially the fine dumplings from Shanghai, dumplings which taste as if they could be Polish or Ukrainian or Japanese but happen to be Chinese, of a Shanghai variety, and nice, very nice. Lots of happy dumplings, still here and there. Pretty much everywhere, really.

So where is my passport? Where is my ID?

These are nice pockets, officer. Soft to touch, like the belly of my pink teddy. And your ID card is here too, next to mine. Let me see. Adam. That's a nice name. Adam Michalowski, born in Lambeth, White British. You have always seemed nice.

So wakey, wakey, Mr. Michalowski. Please, do let me out.

What We Should Feel Now

I want to assure you: you are not what you think we might think. You are not. YOU ARE NOT. Put big signs in your bedrooms. Put a magnet on your fridges. Absolutely not.

There is a chance, of course, I haven't been paying much attention; I don't often put myself first: I have children, jobs, and many other obligations. There are apples rotting in my garden and I need to pick them. But I feel no resentment. I don't think so. Because why? Who did what to me? Thugs? The politicians don't bend down to them to kiss their feet; they put them in prisons, where they belong, surely that's what they do. But I better check this. I better check what I should feel, what my neighbours have been feeling, what everybody is feeling right now, and if they are feeling like they should, like we ought to, like we are told we should feel, or not feel, according to some rule.

"Do you not like me here?" I ask shopkeepers, doctors, policemen, politicians, and friends.

"Of course, don't be silly. We love you. You are like us, you are part of us, you know. Always have. Always will."

"Tell me how I'm like you," I ask.

"For a start, you're busy like us, with children, jobs, and rotting apples in your garden. But let's talk about the weather. It's a little grim here today, don't you think?"

"It's not grim," I say. "It's not grim at all. I love you, I love you. I am putting signs in my bedroom and on my fridge. Signs of love. Little hearts everywhere. Hearts. Big hearts. Love, love, everywhere."

"Love, love everywhere," you repeat. "Love, love, love. Just love. Just love."

We don't feel love right now, but we shake hands. We'll get through this, you say. We'll just get on with it. I say it too. We'll grow new apples together. One day. We'll grow them on pear trees, on flowers, on grass. Anywhere we can find. For next season. Or the season after. For everybody to share and admire, and then we'll all eat together. Our apples. Apples that do not rot.

Making Babies for Great Britain

Aniela didn't want to have babies just yet. And neither did Patsy—of course—because Patsy always copied everything Aniela did. At least, that's what Aniela thought. Patsy copy-cat. Patsy-do-everything-like-Aniela. Patsy-never-ever-do-anything-without-Aniela. She always waited for Aniela, it seemed. Where is Aniela going on holidays? What swimsuit is she bringing? What kind of Victorian house is she buying when she gets back, and with whom? What kind of doors, windows, wallpaper? What flowers in the vase? On what kind of dinner table? For how many people?

When they finally bought Victorian houses—two houses right opposite each other, that is, each with a boyfriend in them—Aniela often imagined her house and Patsy's as two faces, with windows for the eyes and wooden doors for mouths. Patsy's door was bright red and Aniela's was a shade darker; two faces staring at each other all day and night.

Their doors never quite closed, which made Aniela feel she was never alone, because Patsy was almost always within her reach, ready for her, it seemed. Within a few steps. Easy steps. They were always such easy-peasy steps! Light and easy to take. Happy steps!

Then one night, after the wine, Patsy kissed Aniela good-bye. They were both standing on the porch, with the door wide open.

"You are letting the heat out," Ross, Aniela's boyfriend, said.

Patsy shrugged her shoulders and—immediately after her— Aniela shrugged her shoulders too.

"These Victorian houses are drafty, don't you know?" Ross asked.

Patsy just ignored him and went back into Aniela's living room to fetch her handbag, still talking, leaving the front door opened; as if in a half-kiss. She pressed her lips against Aniela's cheek again. "Bye-bye," she said, perhaps wasting everybody's time; the hot air escaping faster and faster from narrow Victorian corridors and halls. But it felt nice, and Aniela didn't mind a bit of fresh air coming in.

"Kiss—and go! Or don't kiss at all," Ross commanded.

Aniela didn't like this tone in his voice. Perhaps he was growing jealous of her friendship with Patsy. Maybe even of their kisses, which he couldn't have; not that often, and so casually.

Aniela often wondered why she and Ross didn't kiss for the sake of kissing anymore. There were times when they travelled somewhere for a day just to kiss for fun and romance, somewhere where they could walk and hold hands; somewhere with no beds and bedrooms; so that they wouldn't forget how it felt to kiss and hold hands, but even that was less and less common now. Or maybe the lack of kissing was simply due to their routine of travelling together less and staying home more, undressing right before bed and sleeping naked, tangled up together—and safely—under their *Hungarian Goose Down Luxury Tog 10*, which Ross referred to as "their cloud." Perhaps kissing and taking off their clothes were unrelated now. A kiss was an invitation, which neither of them needed. Once they became inseparable, under "their cloud," kissing no longer made sense to Ross, obviously. They were both tired from work and the routine of their life together; tired of their bedroom and their duvet; tired of each other maybe, too. And now, he was obsessed with kissing her down there, "French kissing," as he called it. She liked it of course, she liked it very much, but not as much as he did, it seemed. For Ross, it was nice to be so close to a woman, so exciting, it seemed. But she missed traditional ways. She missed the traditional ways a lot. She didn't know why.

She probably kissed Patsy on the lips more often than her Ross these days. Not in the same way—of course. She liked the warmth of Patsy's lips on her cheek, their sudden intimacy, like a whisper in the ear that men could not hear. In the mornings, Patsy's kiss gently woke her up. In the evenings, the kiss confirmed their friendship, the mere fact that Patsy—her neighbour and her super-super friend—was still there for her, even if Ross was at work, getting tired for the evening, getting grumpy for the night, just wanting to hide, under the duvet, and play down there, away from her even though so close.

Then one Saturday, Patsy came knocking at Aniela's door, knocking heavier than usual, which surprised Aniela.

"I locked myself out! Have you got my spare keys somewhere?" Patsy asked.

Aniela couldn't remember where the keys to Patsy's house were. She went and looked in all her cupboards, in her jewellery pot, even in the bathroom cabinet. But she could not find them. It wasn't a big deal, of course. So why was Patsy so anxious? It only meant that Patsy would stay in her house a little bit longer, and would go back as soon as Ron—Patsy's boyfriend—was back.

Ross was out that morning at the car wash. Aniela made Patsy a cup of tea. Patsy looked different, she thought. There was a certain new strength about her, an aura of certainty. Even from the way she knocked it was clear she was sure of something. Patsy always seemed a little lost to Aniela, so this sudden change made Aniela feel weaker; as if Patsy was now the one who would give their relationship a new direction, a push, a lift perhaps; swapping sides with Aniela maybe. Aniela felt a change coming, a certain type of beautiful short-term suffering on its way, which, she hoped, would make their relationship deeper, even if it was Patsy who led it from then on.

Patsy took a sip of her tea, put the cup down, and announced: "I want a baby. But I'm not sure if Ron is ready. In fact, I know he's not. I want a baby with you!"

A baby! Patsy wanted a baby! With Aniela! It was the first time ever that Patsy had initiated something. She seemed ready for it, but Aniela wasn't. Was Ron more ready than Ross? Was everybody suddenly more ready than Aniela?

Ron, in many ways, reminded Aniela of Ross. The men couldn't see beyond the next few days. What was their world about, really? They bonded over football matches, darts, and pints of Guinness. Did they talk about French kissing? Aniela seriously doubted it. They had both lost their mothers as little boys but this never seemed to be interesting to them in any way. It seemed to Aniela that Ross always avoided the subject of *mothers*. Ron and Ross talked about new projects at work or investments. If they talked about the past, it was to recall their glory: the broken elbow that had healed within a week; the money they'd lost and then regained; or their ex-girlfriends who, in their memory, had called their sons baby Ron or baby Ross.

"Have you discussed it?" Aniela asked, thinking that women perhaps bonded in difficulty, they were the closest in pain.

"No. But I thought, wouldn't it be nice: pushing prams—together? Breastfeeding—together? A year off—together?"

And that was it. Aniela didn't need much convincing. She took out her diary and started planning: when was a good time for a baby? Two babies. Their babies.

Ross wasn't really a big part of it—not to start with. She imagined sitting in a park with Patsy and their babies, on a sunny bench—in Mayow Park or, better still, at the Crystal Palace playground. Their kids would learn to crawl together, and then dig holes in the sand. Of all the people she knew, Patsy was the one and only she wanted to go through this with—having fun together, doing lots of nice little things together, like eating ice creams in that lovely round café in Peckham Rye Park—and doing some obviously painful stuff too, like giving birth. But even that seemed like it would be fun with Patsy.

"Are you about to get your period today or tomorrow, like me?" asked Patsy. They were sitting in Aniela's kitchen now, making green tea. They would both have to forget about real tea for a while, of course! Or coffee! Or camembert!

"Yes. You know we always start on the same day."

"Of course! Perfect. So what about if we begin trying a week on Tuesday? Every day? Or every other?"

"Every day, yes, every day." Aniela was excited. Ah, making babies! What fun. What a shame Ron and Ross had to be involved!

Of course, their periods would have ended by then. They would both be ovulating. The calendar was still in her hands, it had all the dates in a red pen. She counted the length of her monthly cycle. Exactly twenty-eight days. How good, how great. She could even do a temperature test, with Patsy.

Then she thought about Ross.

It wasn't that she wanted to use Ross. Of course not! Quite simply, she didn't know how to state it to him, how to ask for something that only Patsy could understand, it seemed.

"Let's make a baby"—that would definitely put him off kissing, she thought.

"The time is just right tonight" was even worse.

"Let's have a family"—that would only stress him out, of course.

So when the following Tuesday came, and every day thereafter, she kissed Ross before bed, and then under "their cloud" she thought of Patsy kissing Ron, and hoped the kissing wouldn't stop too soon for them.

"How is it going?" Patsy asked her the following morning.

"It's going OK," Aniela said. "But he didn't want to kiss back too much. He is just so obsessed with French kissing at the moment. How is it for you?"

"So far, so good," Patsy said. "But I'm worried. He is so careful! Too careful! Only wants to kiss me down there, too, and then it excites him so much that it's just too late for anything else!"

Too late for anything else! Well, that was worrying. Very worrying, and not good news.

"You need to maybe refuse him next time, or say that you're not in the mood, or something," Aniela said, thinking she will have to do the same, exactly the same.

The second night Ross seemed tired but Aniela kissed him and then he wasn't tired after all. They kissed a little more. She imagined Ross and Ron as the same person now, a person whose name starts with "R." R down on her; R opening her legs more and more; R just so excited; R with his head doing little movements; R with his tongue working so hard and then what? Too late, too quickly. R! What a mess! She wanted to shout. What a waste, you know, R, what a mess, and a waste!

"All OK?" Aniela asked Patsy in the morning.

"Hard to say."

They passed a couple of teenagers kissing by Sydenham station. Aniela felt jealous of their deep, passionate snogging.

"She'll be pregnant in no time," Patsy hissed.

It was then that Patsy realised they had to do something to make their boyfriends kiss more on the lips, like getting new bright lipsticks, and then straight to business, with no interruptions, no kissing elsewhere, no way. Just a quick number would do, really, it didn't need to take long at all. They could go down after maybe, if they wished so?

"But how, Patsy, how are we going to force them to do it? What do we change?"

So one day after work they went and bought Rimmel's Matte Finish, to match their wonderful red doors. Aniela's lips—like her door—was now a deeper, darker red than Patsy's. They also got a bottle of red wine each.

That night, having applied lots of lipstick, Aniela kissed Ross and closed her eyes. To her surprise, he didn't pick her up and carry her to "their cloud" at all. She felt a gentle kiss on her left eyelid, and then on her right. Soon, Ross was kissing her entire face, including her nose and ears and even her chin, and it lasted for twenty-five seconds, she counted. She didn't need to explain and ask for him to stay there, just stay there, with his head next to hers. He seemed to understand—without being told—that making babies involved a lot of careful kissing. Thank God. He got that. Or he seemed to have that understanding.

Aniela kept her eyes closed and—in that moment—it felt as if their entire house moved forward across Perry Vale Road to kiss Aniela's house. But then the most annoying thing happened. Ross finished. Just finished. Just like that. Still with his clothes on. Ah, what a waste. What a terrible waste, yet again! Maybe a compliment to her lips, but she wanted no compliments! She wanted babies!

The following day was Friday and she knocked at Patsy's door, in the morning.

"I don't know what to do any more, Patsy. I just want a baby. And he just comes in this useless way! So totally useless for me, and my baby. Comes in his jeans. Or comes on his knees." She felt tears in her throat as she spoke.

Patsy remained collected, and strong.

"Let's walk to the station. I've got an idea."

The day was sunny with lots of tiny little clouds over the city, which looked strong despite being clouds, and tiny. They looked as if they would never disappear, never, from the blue sky. They dotted the sky forever, in a new pattern. The polka-dot sky, like the dress Aniela was wearing today. She liked patterns, especially polka dots, in the sky, and on her dresses.

Today they were the sky. The clouds were the sky.

Patsy looked at the sky too, and then at Aniela's dress.

"Women, we rape," she whispered to Patsy.

"What?" Aniela asked. "Rape?" She was still looking at the clouds, and she thought Patsy is looking at them too, how the soft clouds were covering the big sky more and more, covering the sun, hiding the light; polka dots joining together, creating a big cloud, one strong rain cloud.

"Rape. Yes. We rape."

And Aniela nodded. Just nodded, twice. Of course. They had to rape. How else? This was the only practical solution. The only way out from this oppression!

"Nimbostratus," Aniela said. "Look, that cloud is taking over." She pointed at the sky. "Have you got a spare umbrella?"

"I've got two umbrellas. One for me. And one to rape with," Patsy said and laughed, and Aniela laughed too, and then they laughed and laughed, all the way to the station, and on the train too, and then at work—each at her work, each at her desk—but still laughing at the same joke, laughing more and more, laughing so much they couldn't stop; the laughter now uncomfortable, almost a little painful but quite nice too; a piercing pain going through them. Or maybe it was just proper pleasure, finally surfacing. And more pleasure was coming soon, and by their hands this time.

One Less Button

For sex with Manolo, Bianca went to the Vatican Gardens. For abortions—where the hell in Rome?

She plunged her feet in the Trevi Fountain, flicking back her black mane of hair. Tourists gathered round her. Several fast flashes, as if Bianca was famous, in the great scene from Fellini's film. For a second, she was Anita Ekberg. But her hair was the wrong colour. The wrong length. Wrong—everything.

This is not Fellini. This is Bianca starring in a film by Bianca.

But what would Anita think? What would she do if she was a pregnant Bianca, on a Sunday?

She looked at the tourists again. Of course, Anita wouldn't want the whole of Rome to know how in November it had been so warm, or that the roses in the garden were still in full bloom.

It was nobody's business why her dress had one less button or how Manolo, the Popemobile mechanic, had stared at her and looked so shy.

"How old are you?" he asked.

"Twenty-five," she lied.

Bianca stepped out of the Trevi Fountain and dried her feet on an old Metallica T-shirt she kept in her bag. She then put on her pink Dr Martens.

So where to go and what to do?

Hospitals were for sick people but Bianca felt so healthy! Her home was full of family and guests—it was too loud. So maybe: *the chapel*! So beautiful. Welcoming. Silent and discreet. Like her own body. An ideal place to hide!

"*La cappella di amore*," she called it. Just around the corner from the Vatican Gardens. It was better known to others as the Sistine Chapel. She knew the gardens so well, every flower: the roses, the honeysuckle, and the tulips. The tulips bored her, though. They were not only boring but also sad, with a short lifespan. They only bloomed once a year. The roses were so much more interesting: they bloomed and bloomed, and there was no end to them. Until the gardener deadheaded them, of course, helping them die—a little.

"Taxi," she shouted.

The traffic wasn't too bad on a Sunday. She saw the beautiful dome in the distance, like a cake ready to be eaten. In the chapel, during mass, she could imagine herself as the saint, the bride, or the witch. A full hour of sweet daydreaming—from eleven, on the dot. Although many of her family members always arrived late. Especially her Aunty Maria—the best gynaecologist in Rome.

Walking in, Bianca looked at the ceiling: the two fingers touching, but not quite. She wished she could connect them with a straight, thick line of red paint.

She sat down at the back in the last row, away from her family. They thought of her as a freak anyway, didn't they? Dressed so strangely. Just talking to the plants all the time.

Bianca looked at her Mickey Mouse watch. Quarter past eleven. The chapel was only half-full. Or half-empty?

Suddenly, the doors opened with a loud whoosh. It was Maria. She carried a transparent Gucci bag for her medical equipment: the straps, the cotton sheets, and the portable transvaginal ultrasound scanner, with a monitor attached to it.

She sat next to Bianca, in the last row, her bag taking as much space as another person. Nobody else joined them, of course. Who wants to sit with two witches, in a chapel?

"How are you, my dear?" Maria asked.

"I've got a terrible toothache and headache."

"I'm not a dentist but I could take a look."

The Pope at the altar was so far away that he looked like a figurine, made of china. It occurred to Bianca that maybe he couldn't see them at all. Unless they started jumping up and down, waving their hands like castaways; maybe then he would.

Bianca opened her mouth, discreetly but very wide. As wide as she could.

"I see nothing, but you might want to call the dentist, after the mass. Are you feeling all right?"

Bianca didn't know the answer—with her mouth open, looking at the ceiling—until she realised that she felt cold and shaky and beyond that: nothing.

She looked at the frescoes again. A woman's big thighs. Beautiful people and lambs.

Mickey's hands showed eleven twenty-five. Her throat tickled. She must have caught a cold in the fountain.

There was a confession box right next to them, with a large table behind it, as if the confessed sins would then occupy the guilty space underneath the table.

"So why did you ask me to come here, Bianca?"

"I'm pregnant, I think."

"Why did you not visit me in the hospital?"

"I felt too scared."

"Do you feel scared now?"

Bianca looked down at the rich mosaic, and made a small circle in the air with her foot, copying the pattern of the floor.

"No. I'm not scared." She made another circle, with the other foot.

"Are you ready then, my dear?" Maria pulled the cotton sheet from her bag and put it over the table, forming a little tent. She took her by the arm, like a doctor, rather than an aunty. Bianca looked up the ceiling, at the frescoes. She saw a few horses, here and there.

Inside the tent, they had to talk about something, of course. Bianca whispered: "What's your favourite animal, Maria?"

"I like monkeys. And you?"

"I like sausage dogs."

Bianca sneezed and then coughed.

"Please don't cough now," Maria asked, in her efficient doctor voice.

"Why?"

"Coughing interrupts the whole thing. Sometimes it can even eject probes."

Suddenly, she heard hard steps, fast approaching. Then the wooden gate of the confession box, slamming lightly.

"Shhh," said Maria. "It's the priest! You know, the one with the sausage dog."

She heard a quiet knock from the confession box.

"Now, let me examine you, Bianca, and see if we can terminate."

Bianca thought of Joan, the legendary Popess. Medieval fairy tale for children. Giving birth while riding a horse and better still: exposed and tortured!

No way. Bianca would not have it. She would squash the little fleas in her womb, one by one. She would do it with no consequences, no sadness, not a wink. Surely, it would become her new pleasure, of a kind. A little secret. A compensation. Something extra in her life. She would abort every time—every month—and gain strength from it, and more power, a supremacy—the entire chapel, all full, with time.

"Yes, I wish to terminate it, let's do it, now!" Bianca almost said. But then, her lip trembled and instead she asked: "Where did you get this nice bag, Maria? Was it at the market?"

"Yes, I think it was—the market."

A few minutes passed, but it felt like an hour.

"You can cough now, Bianca. Well done," said Maria.

It was a deep cough. Maybe it was something more serious than a cold: Influenza? Pneumonia?

She looked at her watch. Five more minutes to go. What's that in seconds? Bianca wondered. She couldn't do any maths now.

"Maria? Can I ask you something?"

"Of course, my dear."

"Have you ever decided not to carry on with a pregnancy?"

"Yes. Once."

"And how did you feel?"

"I cried."

In the distance, a baby chuckled loudly. The sound came from the front of the church rather than the back.

Bianca thought about what Maria had just told her. What if, she thought, *sad* wouldn't be how she'd feel. She tried to think of the opposite word for *sad* but *happy* did not quite match it.

Three minutes left. She imagined her watch going much faster—Mickey's hands working hard.

What was Maria doing exactly, for so long, with her baby?

"Do many women change their mind in the middle of the procedure, Maria?"

"Some do. But not if there is a man waiting for them outside, sipping his coffee, reading *La Repubblica*. Sometimes the man lights a cigarette. Sometimes he coughs."

She heard quiet music from above. Bach, she thought. The last piece of music before the end of the service.

Then she thought about her birthday. She would be forty-six, in eight months. What should she have, for her birthday?

"OK, I've got some news for you, Bianca. Let's go back and sit down," Maria said. She folded up her "tent."

It was only a few steps to their row.

"Good news?" Bianca looked up the ceiling: puffy clouds, and half-naked people. Why was everyone so pink and fat, like giant babies?

"It's not great, I'm afraid."

"Not great?" Bianca had never heard any truly bad news before, not for the past forty-six years in fact. Not even when her grandpa Giuseppe died last year. He was ninety-nine and he'd had a full plate of carbonara that day, and a full glass of red too.

Bianca closed her eyes and smelled the sweet scents in the air. That's what they did in films, before the sad news arrived. They seemed to inhale a lot of air.

"The news is about the foetus. I checked three times. It's dead."

Bianca swallowed her own saliva with lots of dry air. It hurt her throat, as if she was trying to gulp down a stone.

"Dead? With no heartbeat?"

"It died. A few hours ago. Or days. Or maybe—a week. No more than two weeks, for sure. That's why my examination took so long. I checked for a baby's heartbeat but there was none! Very *lucky*, in a way."

"*Bambino mio!*" Bianca felt a sharp pain in her tooth, her head beginning to throb hard.

She stepped outside into the colourful garden, a disco dance floor with tulips, roses, and honeysuckle spinning round her. She squinted, felt sick, sat on the grass.

A grasshopper jumped. She looked up.

Next to her, the gardener was pruning the roses. He didn't seem to notice her at all, or hear her loud sobs. With one careful swing of his sharp knife, he deadheaded the rose's smallest bud. Just like that.

One. Beautifully. Clean.

Cut!

A Shit Story

Shit came by the house, unannounced, like a bomb. I was home, with the kids.

"Your wife isn't here," I told him. I don't know why I said "wife." Aunty was no longer married to Shit. It was hard, sitting there, looking at his round face and just accepting him for who he was. Again. Every time he came in fact. My ex-uncle. A terrorist, really, like this terrorist, in our nice lives.

"That's all right," he said. "I'll just wait in the kitchen, Isabelle."

He was four years older than Aunty, and a difficult man, who left her. So it was hard. Hard for me too. Every time. Looking at him and remembering everything, every detail of this awful history. The story was just there, in his eyes now, eyes full of worry and at the same time full of reserved coldness, meanness, madness. His eyes had a smell. They smelled of this rotting blue colour; rotting bubble-gum ice-cream; rotting sweets; rotting teeth eyes. Looking into his eyes was like parachuting into this worry, rot, anxiety land, which had asserted itself in his eyes so much that I now believed that his worry was important, that it had to be addressed, by everyone, by me. It was contagious. In my irises now, and every time I blinked. I was anxious and worried too. So I avoided his eyes, looking into his eyes.

"She shouldn't be long," I said.

He looked at me, and there it was, right in his eyes, dead eyes, reptile eyes. I cheated on Aunty, he said, in effect. I saw prostitutes, and then brought more prostitutes to this house. I then endlessly cheated on prostitutes I had already fucked, just fucked everything, more and more, just so that my own anxiety would not get me, maybe.

"Cup of tea?" I asked.

He nodded, after some time, with a definite delay. He was slower to react than other people I knew, as if he wasn't quite there, sitting in his former chair, in the kitchen, now also our dining room but really still a family kitchen, just with a big hole now, it seemed, or this constant empty, hollow feeling you get after a sudden blast, or a carefully planned explosion. In fact, he sat in his chair like he always used to, leaning forwards, giving an impression of someone listening and caring, like a nice man. He still did it now, the leaning forwards, this pretence of listening, being there, while in fact he wasn't. He was absent, his eyes looked absent, and so did his entire dead face.

"Are you still enjoying living here, in the dining room, now your bedroom, Isabelle?" he asked.

I nodded, but not in agreement. I nodded in order to get it over with. Yes, the dining room was now my room, my bedroom, I nodded again. My nod was telling, I hoped. I moved in with Aunty to give her a hand with the children, because you weren't there, I hoped my nod said. And because it was just so shitty for her; she had such a shitty time. And because she had little money, and nobody wanted to help her. That's why I was still here. I hoped my nod told him all this because of course with Shit you had to say nothing, or he would get even more anxious and explode, and then leave again.

He sipped his tea now and just stared into his cup.

"You are a nice girl, Isabelle, and so very helpful," he said.

"Thank you," I said. But no! I didn't do very much other than just be, of course. Aunty needed that, I think. So I just was, I was, I was, and I took the children to school, and sometimes cooked, did a bit of washing, that sort of thing.

"Are the children OK?" he asked but looked at the cups, looked at the plates; just looked elsewhere.

"Yes, thank you. They are napping now."

Sometimes I did little things for the children. I massaged their feet, sometimes for hours, starting with the toes. Staying with this shit, this difficult situation, was often the most difficult thing and often the most beautiful too, and hopeful. So this disaster happened—it always was a disaster anyway—and we did nothing to clean it up, just lived with it, for a little while. So it continued to be shit, every day.

"Must be nice for the children to be around such a nice aunty," he said.

I didn't respond. I just repeated this sentence to myself, in my head now. Must be nice to be around me.

"Have they been OK?" he asked.

"Yes, thank you."

Occasionally, Olga and Molly still screamed at nights, of course, wetted their beds, developed fears of swimming in an empty pool, or—anxious—didn't sleep at all at night, didn't eat.

"And your aunty?" he asked, meaning his ex-wife of course. He looked away, in an uninterested manner.

"Yes, thank you, she is fine too."

Aunty was still coming to terms with it all. She wanted to do something, every day, at least something very little but she had failed terribly in this, for the past three months, it seemed. Last Sunday, for example, she woke up and got out of bed, and that was it. That was her day's achievement maybe, to be up, not to be in bed for half an hour. Then she went back to bed. Today's achievement was her "journey to the supermarket," as she called it. From these long supermarket trips she often came back empty-handed, and I wondered if she would come back empty-handed today too.

"I like coming here," he said, as if prompted by my lack of reaction. "I like seeing you all, you know, in good health."

Good health, I repeated to myself but said nothing to him. I suppose we were all in good health. And most days, we just had things to do. Work, school, Molly and Olga's quarrels over Lego blocks, and homework, and their little friends too, and their friends' mothers and fathers, who always wanted to know how Aunty was getting on, without offering any real help it seemed, not unless she asked, which was still hard for her, very hard. So really, she did all the things she did when she was married maybe, except now she was getting credit for it, personally, plus she was starting to realise she could ask for help at times. Neighbours whispered: Wow, look at her, Shit left and she is doing so well, holding it all together but of course she held it together before, it wasn't different from before, except now she didn't have to cook for her husband or iron his shirts, and listen to his criticism, and she had more energy suddenly, or a little more, it seemed. So yes, she was healthy. Or not sick.

"Would you like another cup of tea?" I asked.

"No, thank you. One cup is just enough," he said.

I heard a key turning in the keyhole, like a cat scratching in the keyhole, with a sharp claw. Aunty was back. With no shopping.

"Nick is here," I announced, almost saying Shit instead of Nick, and not too loudly, so that the children wouldn't wake up.

"Hello, love," said Shit. He still called her love sometimes.

Aunty walked into the kitchen and looked at Shit. Or rather, she sort of looked above him, above his head. Just above the cooker. This was all she could do, a special non-greeting for him; an acknowledgement that he was there; his head was there, somewhere near her cooker.

"Hello," she said. "The children will be up in a minute."

Shit stood up from his chair. He didn't say anything, as always, no good-bye, or thank you, or whatever you say when you are divorced but want to move from one room to another. I saw him disappearing into the dining room; now my room; my bedroom. Hiding in my bedroom.

I heard the doors shutting behind him quietly, as if bedroom doors deserved a more subtle treatment, even if they were formerly just dining-room doors; always opened, never closed.

"Are you ready?" said Aunty.

I nodded and started getting ready in the kitchen. I put some lipstick on, and my long black boots, and Aunty helped me put my leather coat on.

She looked at me, inspecting every zip, every button, as if getting me ready for school or an important job interview.

"You look nice," she said.

We then heard little Olga and Molly's soft steps like cats' coming down the stairs into the kitchen.

"Is Daddy here, Mummy? I think I heard Daddy's voice?" Molly's cheeks were a little red. She had Shit's eyes. Shit's beautiful blue eyes, but with no madness in them.

"Yes, sweetheart, your daddy is in the dining room," Aunty said.

"You mean Isabelle's room?" asked Olga. She looked a lot more like her mum, with her brown eyes. I could not see Shit in her, not much.

Shit then re-entered the kitchen. He looked scared, like a scared, mad person.

"Hello, Molly. Hello, Olga," he said quietly.

"Hello, Daddy," said Molly.

"Hello, Daddy," repeated Olga.

Shit gave them each a big hug. They hugged for a long time.

"Right, have fun with Daddy, and Mummy and I will go for a little walk, in the park. What time do you want us to be back, Nick? What time do you need to leave?" I asked.

Shit looked at his watch but said nothing, as if he had forgotten how to tell the time, on his watch. Aunty just stood there too, not ready to go anywhere, distressed by the sight of the children—her children—hugging Shit. They were her children now, she often said to me. Shit did not deserve to see them now, she whispered, so that nobody heard, just me. She said that crying, sobbing, between the lines. This was the hardest thing for her now, to vacate the house for these unexpected hours, whenever he came, even if she'd only just got back herself, just to give them some space, and time, to see each other. Just so Shit could continue pretending to be Father, to see the new toys, new books, give the children the bath. But maybe it was unfair. He was Father. Of course he was still Father. And Father was important. Very important. For girls. But no longer her husband. It was so brave of her, I thought, so brave of her to leave, just leave him to it, to trust, when no trust was left.

"But why, Mummy? But why do you always have to leave when Daddy comes?" Olga's eyes looked wet, angry and wet, with her angry tears. "Why can't you stay with us?"

Shit just stood there in the middle of the kitchen, and Aunty, too, just stood, helpless. How much longer can we go on like this? I thought. With this fucking small talk, pleasantries, pretending and more pretending, to each other, to the children. Protecting the children, or harming the children. Harming the children with our small talk, the pleasantries, and the lies, white lies, like they are stupid, like they can't see anything for themselves, for fuck's sake.

I looked at Olga and Molly, who maybe wetted their beds sometimes but coped so well, maybe coped better than Aunty and Uncle Shit. Because they were both so shit, just shitty parents. Both of them despairing, in their own heads, hurt and hurting, no longer aware of who is hurting who more, with what, to whom, with whom, and why, and what. It didn't matter to me now, who was the victim, and who not, and why not. They just weren't together any more, and that was it. It wasn't that bad, was it? So why not just tell the children, I thought?

"I'll tell you why," I said. "It's because your Mummy and Daddy are no longer together. But Daddy wants to see you, so the best thing to do is for us to just leave you to it, you know? Just give you some time, together. You know, it's like we all need to get to know each other again. All over again. Because Mummy and Daddy are no longer married. And you are not part of that marriage. Marriage is just two people. They will always be your Mummy and Daddy, though. No matter what."

"It's not that," said Shit. "This is not why she is crying." He was suddenly awake, more awake. This was part of his madness, to explode just as things were settling. To have some new idea to drop on us.

"Why is Olga crying then, in your opinion?" I asked.

"She is upset with your language. Just the way you say things. Not what you say, but how. You talk to her as if you didn't like me."

I looked at him. "Well, it is true. I don't like you very much, Nick, at the moment. But that's just me. I don't expect the children to do the same. In fact, I expect the children to love you, I really do, even if it's difficult for me to feel that sometimes, to accept this new situation. To love you, as my uncle."

I looked at Aunty. She was just staring at the cooker. Above the cooker, below the cooker, then next to it, as if she was looking for another kitchen appliance. Another kitchen appliance was missing from her kitchen maybe.

"Yes, I noticed that," said Molly. "Daddy and Isabelle don't like each other at the moment very much." Molly was nodding now, like a grown-up.

"I don't know what I have done, to you, Isabelle," said Shit. "Or your Mum."

Aunty coughed now, nervously. It was the kind of cough that announced she wasn't going to be involved in this at all, that she was just nervous, and that I was all alone here, talking to him.

"I don't think I ever liked you, very much," I said. "I never thought you were a particularly nice man. Or had anything interesting to talk about. But that's just me, I guess." I looked at the children now. "I don't have to like Daddy, you know. Even if you do."

"Yes," Aunty said. Yes meaning what?

Olga stopped crying. She looked intrigued, in fact. Animated, happy.

"But I want Isabelle to like Daddy," said Olga, laughing.

"Well, at the moment I just can't. I need time. Some time."

"Yes," Aunty said. "She needs time maybe."

"Yes," I continued. "I just don't think Daddy is very interesting, is all. You can still love your Daddy, of course, even if I say I don't find him interesting. Even if he doesn't live with us, you know. It's still allowed, to love him, and give him lots of hugs. As many as you like. He is your Daddy."

Shit looked angry now. Was it anger? Or madness, more madness because I said he was not an interesting man maybe, to me? To Molly and Olga it didn't matter much, it seemed. They took Shit's hand—both held him by the same hand—and dragged him up the stairs to their room, to show him a new toy, a new book, a new something, and I heard laughter for the first time in months, and more laughter, even Shit laughing now, at something, it didn't matter what, as we were going out now. We needed to be out.

Daddy Fox

"Come into the kitchen," said Louise.

The fox walked slowly, looking around like a hurt animal. He entered the kitchen. "Thanks, Louise," he said. "You're too kind." His tail ended with a stump, and he dragged it along the floor like a wooden leg. Louise listened to the hollow sound of his tail against the dark terracotta floors. She wondered if he ever experienced phantom pain, like an amputee.

"Does your tail ever hurt?"

"Yes, especially at night. It hurts at the very end—the missing end. Here," he pointed at the tail. He had a Midwestern accent. Either Michigan, or Wisconsin. Not very strong. Similar to her Uncle Steven's, who went hunting for elk every October.

"Light, where is the light?" he asked. He had beautifully shiny fur but smelled like a human. He sounded like Uncle Steven when he said "light." The way he repeated "light" twice, in one sentence. Steven, too, talked about the light, as well as saints, devils, pregnant virgins, and the process of taxidermy. As a child, she refused to sit on Uncle Steven's lap when he dressed up as Santa for Christmas, or a giant Easter bunny in spring.

The light switch felt cold on her fingers.

"That's better, with the *light*," said Daddy Fox. "Denis asleep?"

Louise looked at the radiant bulb. She couldn't decide on the colour of the chandelier when they first moved in, so they never bought one. Whenever they argued, Louise took Denis to the kitchen. It was enough for her to put the interrogatory light on—to make him say "sorry" more quickly. Often, he would say "switch off the damn light" long before they even had an argument. They never argued like a husband and wife, it occurred to her. More like siblings. She was the older sister, surely.

"Why is it better with the light? I know my kitchen so well I could cook with my eyes closed."

"I can see you better now, Louise," Daddy Fox said. "Besides, light is important. Light means a lot to me."

"I keep calling you Daddy Fox, but surely—that's not your name?"

It felt strange to have a fox in the house. There was a part of her that would have liked to lock the fox in the kitchen, or under the stairs, and show it to Steven. But Steven was a day and a half away from her. He only came to fix things, it seemed. Once or twice a year. He fixed things so that they would not have to talk. Replacing broken tiles, putting pictures up, painting walls.

"I don't have a name. Everybody calls me Daddy."

"What were you called before you became Dad?"

"I was called Son."

"Are you no longer somebody's son then?"

"I'm Dad. To you, too. Just call me Dad. Or Father."

She looked at his tail again. It was moving up and down, and to the sides. So maybe it wasn't entirely dead. She wondered how he had lost his tail. It was pinkish at the very end—like raw meat.

Pink, it occurred to her. Pink looked good with brown. It brightened the place up. Maybe that's what they needed in the house—more pink.

"Is that what your wife calls you? *Father*?

"Yes, Mother calls me Father too."

"And your son?" She saw their brown plates drying on the rack. A few pink plates—that would be nice. Or a pink rack? Not hot-hot but naturally deep, like the inside of her mouth or her tongue when, after brushing, she mixed a teaspoon of sea salt with freshly boiled water and rinsed her gums to harden them up, so that they would not bleed. Her gums might bleed even more in pregnancy, she thought.

"My son calls me Pete."

"So you have a name then?"

"It's a special name—that only my son can use, Louise."

"I won't use it then. But I'll remember it. I'll say it in my mind— to myself—so that you cannot hear."

The fridge opened with a familiar key, like the beginning of a Brahms symphony.

"I'd rather you called me Father—in your mind too. If you ever think about me."

"Father. I haven't said *father* for years, you know."

"When do you think of me, Louise?"

"I don't think of you very much. But when I do—it's when I cook. Or when I try to fall asleep and you howl outside. Now that I think I'm pregnant, I think about you more. Do you like what I cook?"

"Do you cook a lot, Louise?"

"I do—do you like it?"

"I'd like to watch you cook one day."

"I don't like it when people watch me. I get embarrassed. I never let anyone in the kitchen when I cook. I get very hot when I cook. Especially now—with the baby." She touched her stomach but felt nothing. "I feel hotter." She looked up at the ceiling, her hand still on her stomach. The light bulb was like the torso of a woman—all bright.

"I won't embarrass you. And yes, I like what you cook."

"What's your age, Daddy Fox? In human years?"

"I'm thirty-eight."

He looked up. "It's very bright—this kitchen. I like bold, bright kitchens. Nothing to hide."

"The stove needs scrubbing. The sink needs descaling. The water's so hard."

"I'm hungry. Do you want me to leave the kitchen while you prepare my food, Louise? Or can I stay? Just wave at me if it gets too much. Say 'shoo'—as if I was a dog."

"OK. Let's try. What would you like?"

"A Spanish omelette."

"How many eggs?"

"Four. Ouch. Sorry. The tail. It always hurts more when I'm hungry."

She opened the fridge again. "I've only got three."

His eyes were now closed, his tail curled up as if in pain. Then his eyes opened wide, with a sudden relief, it seemed.

"Better now. Much better, Louise. The pain sort of comes and goes. Let's eat."

Ring burner on, like a miniature bonfire. She took off her cardigan. The wool made no sound as it landed on the kitchen floor. He folded the sweater neatly, with his teeth.

"How did you lose your tail?"

"In a fight."

"With a dog?"

"No, a man. A wise man. I was stupid."

The eggshells were dappled with small black dots. She placed all three in her hand. She could hold four—or five—if she wanted. Easily. Maybe she could even juggle them in the air.

A loud crack. A yolk. Yellow and pulsating with life.

The omelette sizzled as she flipped it over.

"Daddy, here you are."

The Afterlife of Trees

My twin sister Lucy left a suicide note. All it said was: "Merry Christmas."

It must have hurt the palm tree to carry Lucy's weight for the whole night, with her feet dangling in the air, bending the trunk in a perfect arch but not quite reaching the other side.

Our mum didn't make a scene. She knew what to do. First, Lucy was taken away. Then it was time to look at the damage to the palm tree. It looked like it might have been slightly broken in the middle.

"Will it survive till Christmas?" asked Mum. It was hard to tell whether she cared about the palm tree more than her oak trees, or the apple trees. Perhaps she was curious to see it fight for life.

Mum then asked me to send a text message to everyone in Lucy's mobile contact list: "Lucy Sanders. Deceased. Please remove from your database." She inspected the palm tree again and asked me to water it. I went into the garden looking for the watering can. I almost called for Lucy to help me find it.

The next day Mum wanted to know if I needed any of Lucy's clothes. I looked through her wardrobe. I took her Reiss trousers.

Mum didn't try to understand Lucy's reasons for taking her own life. "People have the right to live or die," she announced. "The drive to die is as strong as the drive to live, or perhaps it's part of the same thing, like love and hate." Obviously, she had seen her own parents, husbands, and friends buried and re-buried; when we moved from Kraków to Plymouth, she asked for Dad's grave to be moved with us. I wonder if she felt that death was part of life, like food and water. It was the trees that puzzled her more, I think.

"Trees never really die," our mum used to say when we were little. "Even if you think they die on the surface, the roots are often good and strong." She would sometimes cut whole trees down to see if they could grow back months later—and often they did.

Mum never told us which trees were her favourite. It was hard to tell if she preferred the weak ones or the strong, the ones with leaves or spikes. When a tree really did die, to the roots, she would dig it out and burn it. "A waste of space," she used to say. And yet she would often inspect the holes left by the dead trees, as if they might tell her secrets.

Her cottage was ideal for two people. It had two bedrooms, two bathrooms, and two armchairs by the TV set. I decided to move in with her till after Christmas.

One frosty morning, a couple of days before Christmas, I noticed that the palm tree was now covered in sleet. Its three remaining yellow leaves were half-eaten by slugs, and I wondered if the tree would survive till the festive season or die like Lucy.

I had my own plastic Christmas tree, a few baubles, a set of Ikea cups, a wok, and some other kitchen utensils. They fitted in seventeen boxes which I had placed in the far corner of the kitchen. I moved a couple of boxes into the living room.

I found the box with my plastic Christmas tree. I opened the box and placed the tree next to the window. It had beautiful red lights. With a few more decorations it looked perfect, better than the real Christmas trees that Lucy had insisted on purchasing every Christmas, placing them in the opposite corner of the room, in everyone's way. I couldn't wait to show it to our mum. I knew Lucy would have HATED it. *What* would she say to me? *How* would she say it? I tried to form a sentence, a quick snappy reply like her suicide note but my memory of the sounds was completely gone. I couldn't replicate them. Each time I opened my mouth, I heard my own breaking voice. Was I forgetting her already? So soon? I turned on the radio and began tuning it, hoping to hear the familiar timbre.

"Why the fuck did you put it by the window? It should go in that corner," I heard. The voice was coming from the garden and sounded like my sister's.

I opened the back door.

"Lucy? Is that you?"

Nobody answered. The garden looked empty, with only the sad palm tree in the middle looking even frailer than before, bending in the wind as if it needed a large walking stick to hold it straight. I turned around and went back into the house locking the doors behind me.

"Like I said: not here—there."

The voice was now coming from near the radio. I then saw Lucy standing by the table, pointing her finger at the tree. The Christmas tree slowly lifted up above the floor. With a quiet swish, it levitated across the room.

"Look, I don't need you to tell me where to put my Christmas tree! Go away!" I shouted, realising we had always screamed at each other. I opened the box labelled "kitchen utensils." I saw the handle of the wok, so I took it out.

Lucy readjusted a golden paper bird at the very top of the Christmas tree; it was my favourite decoration, a gift from our mum for Christmas, fifty-seven years ago.

"Lucy, please go now, before Mum wakes up," I pleaded. The back of my sister reminded me of the palm tree outside: tall, her grey hair like long leaves. But she didn't even look at me. She took the paper bird off the tree and ripped it into shreds.

I stood behind Lucy. Then I raised my hand into the air and brought the wok down on her head. The wok vibrated like a gong.

Lucy scratched her head as if a mosquito had just bitten her. Letting herself out through the back door, she spread the pieces of golden paper over the garden like confetti.

I lifted the Christmas tree with one hand and moved it towards the window, where it had been before, the wok still shaking in my other hand.

Mum walked in leaning against her Zimmer frame. She took the wok from my hand. She then moved into the kitchen.

"There," she hung it on a nail above the cooker. "Best place for it."

I looked at the palm tree outside, its leaves green and lush.

Los Lutones

Miles's face looked very, very red. And so did his neck. If his body had a smell, it would be of a building on fire.

"Stop playing bloody jazz, Vito. Forget about jazz!" His neck became whiter now but only by a tinge. "You need to become a Latin band instead. Rebrand. Make money. Do you understand about money? Lots of money? If you haven't become Amy Winehouse by now, Vito—with *her* fucking money—you never, never will."

Suddenly, Miles's cheerful pink office, in the heart of Luton, became a different kind of space. In an instant, the words made everything darker and heavier for Vito. Because Miles didn't just talk about "never." It was a "never, never." Vito's future no longer pink but brown, for ever and ever.

"Amy Winehouse? But she was a girl," was all he managed to say, though it didn't really matter because Vito was gay, so he liked girls.

"Exactly, Vito. And who knows. Maybe it was jazz that killed Amy Winehouse in the end."

"Jazz?" he wanted to ask. "Jazz killed?"

But instead he said: "Okay, Miles" because he, too, had bills to pay and he wanted to both make a living, and live. He wanted to live because to die was a luxury. He couldn't afford an agent who would want to die with him, for classy jazz. And really, deep down, Vito wanted to find someone. Someone nice to be with. Someone to die for. Someone to die with. Someone who loved jazz.

The next morning, Vito woke up to the sound of a text message alert on his phone. The message said: "My mate Carlos. He needs you for tonight. Five grand. Cash-in-hand." Except it wasn't a local gig in Luton. It was in West Yorkshire. No jazz, of course, but Latin music. For a local political party's convention. Vito didn't catch the name of the party. He just kept thinking, is that what people want? Like this is fucking Spain? Like we have bloody sunshine? And no rain? Just cheerful kind of music?

But Los Lutones were fine about it. Totally fine. Maybe because Vito told them they didn't need to change their name. The name was always kind of Latin anyway.

Vito set off early. Like super early. Before his morning piss. He stopped their van for coffee, and a toilet break. Vito only noticed then how urinals came in fours.

Los Lutones stood next to each other but Vito wanted to be fair. He didn't look higher than the streams. He really tried.

Frankie couldn't urinate if anyone stared at him anyway. John's wee-wee was almost orange. He was addicted to his soluble Seven Seas, which he drank with a shot of vodka each morning. It wasn't because his girlfriend was Polish. He just liked it that way. Luke's was brownish. And hardly any. Vito asked him why. He just shrugged. But Vito's stream was strong, always so strong.

He finished first too. "Come on, boys." The zip felt cold in his hands.

After an eight-hour drive, they finally reached Hot Heaven. They found the marquee with "Mexican Night" written on it.

Inside was all white, like somebody's wedding: tables covered with white cloth, white carnations in white vases. And lots of white people. Only white, in fact. White, from another planet. Vito couldn't decide: Were all these golden chains nice or did they look too heavy; was the make-up just right, or too bold on their small thin faces; their skin faking a tan, or was the tan OK, really? They all looked a bit like Mum, or her sisters and brothers. Maybe they were a different race, it occurred to Vito. Not white but tanned white. White, with orange bits. Kind of nice, really. Different.

A few people from the caravan park were now peeking through the hole in the marquee: their three heads formed a perfect triangle. Then a man and a woman walked in through the main entrance. They were dressed in tight white jeans. Vito couldn't tell their ages. They were one of those couples that stayed young forever. Pixie and Dixie. They were holding hands. They could have been anything from thirty-five to sixty-five. And happy. In their little world. Very little world.

A man followed them in. He was a giant. He looked a bit like George Clooney. Middle-aged but still handsome. The always-handsome-no-matter-what variety of handsome. Different. Different to what, say, Americans might think when they think of Great Britain, for sure. They think of the Queen. They think of David Bowie. But he was kind of American, from Kentucky maybe, or Texas, confident in an American way. But British.

He shook Pixie's and Dixie's hands. He was different. Different from Pixie and Dixie. Different from different.

When he finally said: "I'm Carlos," to Vito, it sounded like he was from Luton, with a light Benidorm twang.

Los Lutones began their best number first. It was for Carlos; for the man and the woman in white jeans; for the few heads at the hole. It was a slow-slow, fast-fast, slow-slow, fast-fast salsa tune. A classic. The couple began dancing. One of the heads in the triangle started swinging up and down. Carlos was like a rock.

After a few bars, Carlos waved towards them like you do when a lorry is about to crash into you.

"What's this?" he shouted. The couple stopped dancing. They stopped playing. The heads disappeared from the hole.

"Salsa," Vito said to the microphone.

"Turn off your mike when you are speaking to me."

"Salsa," Vito's voice sounded a lot weaker now.

"It's supposed to be a Mexican night, right? Didn't Miles tell you?"

"No, sir. He said 'Latin'. Does it matter? These people were dancing."

"Does it matter? Jesus. Come to my caravan, straight away."

He then whistled to the DJ. In an instant, "Here Comes the Sun" filled the darkening room. Pixie cheered.

Carlos's caravan was at the other end of Hot Heaven, between a shop and a Wash-N-Dry. It had a large oak desk and not a single chair.

Carlos sat down on his desk.

"You boys are good at what you do. But it's not working, is it?"

He pointed at a yellow line where the carpet ended and the bare floor began. "Line up. Introduce yourselves."

One by one, they lined up.

"Los Lutones: I'm Vito—the frontman. John—bass. Luke—timbales. Frankie—trombone."

"Are you a Cuban or a Mexican band then?"

Vito wanted to say "Latin," but he realised this word for some reason really upset Carlos, back in the tent. So instead he said: "Cuban. From Luton. We are a ... salsa band. We played at Mexican gigs before, though," he lied. "We just wore ... Mexican hats."

"Mexico," Carlos pointed at one part of the room. "Cuba," he pointed at the opposite side. "You guys have no idea."

"I know. The difference is huge. Look—our agent must have got it wrong."

"It's your fault, Vito." Carlos got up from his desk.

"Hold on. I'm sure I've heard of Mexican salsa." Now Luke was trying to reason with the big man, it seemed.

"Yeah, in Nandos. It's called *salsa picante*. A dip made of to-matoes, onions, and peppers." Carlos's voice was getting louder, with a stronger Benidorm twang.

"Sounds delicious," Luke said. Vito thought of Luke's brownish urine, back in the toilet.

"What do you know?" Carlos's face turned red. He didn't look like George Clooney anymore. "Jesus, it's hot here." He wiped his forehead.

"Vito—you talk. The rest of you—shut up. Please." After "please," he was back to his more elegant Clooney self again.

"Yeah, shut up, like Carlos said," Vito could always say "sorry" to Luke later. The brown wee-wee worried him now. Maybe Luke wasn't well? But he was huge, in every way. Did large mean "healthy?"

"So you wore Mexican hats and nobody could tell?" Carlos looked at his watch.

"*Nadie*," Vito struggled to remember a single word in Spanish.

"Your Spanish is pretty good." Carlos looked impressed.

"I lived in Spain for a year. I picked up a few words here and there—enough to sing a song or two... Also, my dad was Italian. Or so my mum tells me."

"OK. Let's do it. Let's find you boys some nice hats."

He took them around the park to another caravan full of clothing. There were bras to fit a little cow, Victorian dresses, a leather horsewhip, and red stilettos.

Vito winked to Luke. But Luke looked away. "Hey man," Vito said. Luke turned his back to him. Strong spine.

"No more hats. We've given them all out." Carlos kicked the whip. It landed by Luke's feet.

"Would it help if we started with… 'La Cucaracha'? That's Mexican, right?" Vito imagined Carlos's perfect stream of urine, stronger than Vito's, so much stronger.

"You know that song?" Carlos's teeth were a bit yellow but he had a good smile: broad, sincere, and full of promise. Vito wondered how Carlos had ended up where he was, in a caravan park. Maybe he was hiding something.

"Yup. We also know 'Bésame Mucho.'"

"You do, Vito—we don't." Luke kicked the whip back at Carlos. But Carlos only smiled at Vito.

"What else can you play? Tell me. What's your favourite tune, Vito."

"It's 'Waltz for Debbie', actually."

"Ah, I love that song," he said. "I so love it. Classy jazz number!" He looked at Vito again and smiled. "Oh, how I wish you guys could just play a bit of jazz tonight. But of course you can't, can you? And all these people, they don't know what's good for them. Mexican night. In Britain. Makes no sense. Only jazz is for Britain. And I can tell you that, as an outsider. An outsider—even for the outsiders. Cup of tea anyone? Milk? Sugar?"

Hard sugar, but still sugar. And very sweet. And it would slowly melt, Vito decided.

"Have you got any tequila? And can we all have a little shot? It's been a long drive," said John. He looked desperate for his drink of soluble vitamins with vodka, actually.

"Of course." Carlos took out a lime from his pocket.

"Remember that Mexican number we did last year, at the Jazz Festival? What was it called?" Outside Vito googled "Danny Rodriguez" on his phone. No, not "Danny." It was "Tommy."

"Wasn't it just called 'Jazz in Mexico'?" Luke was on his phone, too. Funny, the way he held his phone, like a tool—a fork or a knife—and not like a phone.

"Yes, it was a good one. Latin jazz!" Frankie's phone was huge, more like a mini iPad.

John didn't have a phone so he just stood there, empty-handed, with a smile on his face, like a girl. Kind of nice, really.

Then Carlos came and inspected everyone's phone, from behind. "Yeah, that's what I mean. This is what I call *Mexican*."

Then they found the hole in the marquee where Vito had first seen the three heads. All five of them, including Carlos, looked inside. Good turnout: at least a hundred people, all wearing Mexican hats. Vito spotted the couple in the white jeans. They were sipping tequila from the same glass—with two straws. A DJ on the stage was doing a good warm-up, with a Boy George number.

The grass felt still warm from the sun when Vito put his phone down. Los Lutones gathered round it. First track on. Everybody humming along.

Carlos stayed outside the circle. He seemed in a mood again. "I know better versions of this number. The singer sounds Venezuelan." He kicked a little stone towards the marquee.

Suddenly, it became clear to Vito that no music could ever be good enough for Carlos unless he was somehow involved in it.

"Do you want to have a go?" he asked Carlos. "Please, suggest a track, and then we'll play it. For you."

Vito felt Carlos's strong arm around him, and his soft voice in his ear. "Jazz in Mexico," he whispered. Vito then closed his eyes and just listened because Carlos's voice was nice, deep, and a bit like Amy Winehouse's. Then Luke joined in humming again. The rest of the boys began to stamp their feet to the rhythm, their arms tightly around each other.

Then Carlos continued to sing like a million pounds, which is more than a million dollars. A little more. And Vito just loved him for it. More and more, faster and faster, and sometimes quite slow.

Fox Season

Konrad's eyes were like the Dunajec River full of rainbow trout. His teeth—tiny blocks of white Lego.

"When I was little, my father took me fishing. We went everywhere: Zakopane, Gdynia, Sopot. Every night he brought home worms, in a plastic box, and put them on the dinner table." Konrad, too, placed a glass jar next to the salt and pepper. "They were big Polish worms, Emilia, red Californians. These are smaller. From Richmond Park."

"Richmond Park? You went all the way to Richmond Park just to find a couple of worms?" Through the thick glass, Emilia saw a baby worm wriggle its way up the jar. "For God's sake. Not on the dinner table, Konrad! Put them away!"

"Calm down, Emilia. You are scaring the children."

She closed her eyes and counted to ten. The dining room smelled of trout, baked cheese, prawns, hardboiled eggs, and earth. She looked at the fish pie on her plate. It was hard to say if the white bits were pieces of egg, potato, or trout. They were all shades of white. Whitish.

"Are Polish worms better than English ones, Daddy?" Lola was seven. She had Baltic blue eyes, with black eyelashes which curled at the ends like sharp hooks.

"Well, you know what my father used to say? 'All worms speak the same language to the fish.' He also told me a man should learn to wait for his fish. This was the most important lesson I learned from my father. Patience and where to find good worms to catch medium-sized trout. Oh, how he loved fish! We had it every day. For breakfast, lunch, and supper."

Emilia shifted the jar to the furthest corner of the table. "And how was your day, Konrad? Did you write anything? And was it—good?"

"I think I've cracked that poem. You know the war poem. It now ends with soldiers marching out of Warsaw, rather than bombs exploding in the countryside. Works much better… Lola, stop pulling faces at Olek. You are only provoking him. Olek, stop hitting Lola. Sit down, both of you!"

"Can I wash my hands, *Tatusiu*?"

"Lola, you've just washed your hands."

"But they are still sticky, *Tatusiu*. Sticky from the soap."

"*Nie!* Sit down and listen to me. It's dinnertime. It's family time. No running around. Understood?"

There was a distant screeching noise a few streets away, like a baby crying. And then another. A quick pause and then a long howl, as if in Morse code. The foxes are on their way, Emilia thought.

"What's for dessert, Mummy?" Lola licked her plate.

"Indian sweets from the Patels. It's Diwali tonight."

"I thought it was Halloween."

"Halloween's in two weeks."

The last piece of fish pie sat in the centre of Olek's plate. He looked presidential sitting in his chair, like his Polish grandpa, who always wore a suit and a tie, even when he went fishing. Olek kept the family together. Even when he was just three months old, he had kept the family together.

Cling-clang. And more cling-clang. Four white plates—all empty again.

Right—dessert, Emilia thought.

Back in the kitchen, she put jalebi, balls of gulab jamun and soft cushions of rasgulla onto a large brown plate in the shape of a fish. It occurred to her that there was too much brown in their house—not just the plates but also the table, the curtains, the bookshelves, even the edges of the books. The brown seemed to drag down the white walls.

She had once seen a small farmhouse in Zakopane, with a very small kitchen. It had nothing inside—just white walls like theirs, and tiny beds. A large wooden cross on the wall. The house had looked empty, as if the people were still moving in. The family had been living there for over fifty years.

"Never believe in people's nationality, it means nothing," Mother had once said. "Look at their houses and judge them by what they eat. Don't look at the size of their kitchens."

Sometimes she wished Mother was still alive to discuss the world and the meaning of things with her. Mother would have laughed. "Kids are brilliant. That's all that counts."

"Smells like bubble gum," said Lola and swallowed the last piece of jalebi from her small, brown plate.

The plates, the cups, and even the forks and knives seemed heavier than usual when Emilia carried them into the kitchen. In the kitchen, Olek squirted the plates with lemon-scented washing-up liquid.

"So sweet," he said, "like another dessert. Can we always buy this kind, Mum?"

"I like the pomegranate-scented washing-up liquid more, Olek. I think this one really doesn't smell like lemons."

"But I like the smell, Lola. It's like citrus sorbet." Olek leaned over the kitchen sink.

"Are you still hungry, son?" Emilia scooped the leftover fish pie into a plastic bowl. Konrad's large warm hand rested suddenly on hers.

"Why don't you put the leftovers in the fridge? I could have it for lunch tomorrow."

"I can't. The fridge is full of your worms, Konrad."

"It's not."

"It is.

"Let me have a look." He opened the fridge.

"I don't want my food next to your worms, Konrad. They smell."

"Smell of what?"

"They smell of dirt."

"Give the fish pie to the damn foxes then." He slammed the fridge door. He then patted the fridge as if to say, "Sorry."

It occurred to Emilia that poets should not fish. Maybe Konrad wasn't really a poet. "Real" poets didn't spend Sundays digging for worms, being outdoorsy. Poets wrote, using all their senses, and engaged with the world. They saved countries. They didn't like to eat, surely. They were thin, like Emilia's father, who hadn't been a poet. He had been a cheese merchant but maybe a poet nonetheless. Being a little hungry would help Konrad, surely.

"You said *damn* Daddy. You said it at Mummy." Lola had a big smile on her very pretty face. "*Damn* is a swear word. Olek doesn't know it yet."

"I know it now."

"Daddy is swearing at Mummy, Olek. Look—they are arguing."

"Sometimes parents need to argue, Lola. We are sorting the fridge out, that's all. Daddy is just discussing things with Mummy."

"But please, *Tatusiu*."

"OK. Last time. Let Mummy feed them."

The glass doors made a sound like a musical saw when Emilia slid them open. Outside she felt the cold wind on her neck. The lights on the porch clicked.

"Good evening," she said, backing up a few steps. Two wild little eyes glowed in the dark through a hole in the fence. Emilia put the bowl in the middle of the lawn.

Daddy fox was first through the hole. He had beautiful shiny fur and kept his head high. He tried a bit of her fish pie, licked his mouth and looked round. Maybe it was a sign for the rest of the family. Almost immediately *Mamusia* fox arrived too. She was heavily pregnant, taking every step with slow elegance and caution. A couple of steps behind daddy fox—but not really.

What a perfect couple, Emilia thought.

What a perfect family.

Returning to the house, Emilia slid the doors closed. She felt Konrad's strong arm around her back; a quick hug that she wished had lasted longer. Olek's soft head against her elbow felt good too; Lola's warm fingers—around her waist.

"I told you she was pregnant," she whispered to Konrad or maybe to herself.

"She can't be. Foxes don't give birth in winter, Emilia."

"They are town foxes, Konrad. They have accidents. They don't have to hunt like country foxes. They have more time on their hands."

"Are they in love, like you and Daddy?"

"They must be, Olek, if they are still together in the same garden."

"Why in London? Why in town?" Lola stood up on her toes to see better.

"The coyotes won't get them here—that's why." Olek's head pressed harder against Emilia's elbow.

"That's stupid. There are no coyotes in England, Olek."

"Damn. Look, Lola, he's crawling."

"Of course it's crawling, Olek. It's a fox. It can't walk on two legs."

"Kids, time for you to go to bed." Konrad yawned showing his Lego teeth again.

The next day was Saturday.

"Fancy Chinese?" asked Konrad while he poured a glass of Chardonnay for Emilia in the kitchen. The kids never liked Chinese stir-fries, it seemed. They were OK with steamed dumplings; maybe they reminded them of Polish *pierogi*.

The foxes liked *pierogi* too, thought Emilia.

Their Volvo was dark and silent as they drove through the dark and silent streets. They parked in front of the restaurant. It was almost empty, and smelled of freshly cooked rice.

Emilia looked at Konrad's hands: giant paws holding matchsticks. The waiter was tall and muscular, with a screechy voice. More like a Kazakh, Emilia thought.

"Have you got larger size of chopsticks? Say, twice as long?" Konrad put his hands under the table, as if embarrassed.

"There are people with big hands in China, too." The waiter looked at his own hands: not super large but with long fingers. Emilia heard Konrad swallow his Peking duck—he would not hear her now, not every word, not the important bit, not for another few minutes.

Sitting next to them was a beautiful mixed-race woman, in an orange dress, on her phone.

"Eric is teething again," the woman said into her phone.

"Isabella can swim under water—"

"Julia is starting school next September—"

Emilia tried to guess their ages. She thought about the names. Eric, Isabella, and Julia.

Eric—she liked Eric.

On their way home, the headlights of the passing cars made her think of the fox's eyes. Konrad drove slowly.

"Mummy, am I mixed-race?" asked Lola.

"No, you are White Other."

"I don't want to be *other*. I want to be *normal*."

"You are *normal*," Konrad's grip on the wheel got visibly tighter.

"You are *stupid*. So *stupid*."

"Olek! Be nice to your sister. Let's go. The foxes must be getting hungry." Emilia closed her eyes. If only they could be quiet for a minute. Just one minute. No more than that.

"You aren't feeding them tonight, Emilia?" Konrad stopped at the traffic lights. Red—so much redder in the dark.

"I might make them a quick meal, Konrad. Bacon and eggs. Or maybe pancakes."

"Are you crazy? Why don't you feed them my worms?"

She imagined a baby fox with a fat wriggly worm in its mouth. Her stomach began cramping.

"Can you open all the windows?" Had she gulped down her food too quickly?

"Why? Are you hot?" He turned up the air conditioning.

"Stop the car!"

His side window went down. Cold wind, and more cold wind. Cold—but not refreshing.

"I'm going to be sick. Stop!"

He hit the brakes. She staggered out. She felt his warm hands on her forehead. She didn't want him to watch but she didn't want him to go away.

They returned to the car and drove back in silence.

Two weeks left till Halloween, she thought. The children will go trick-or-treating. Konrad might leave a box of sweets on the doorstep and make sure that the foxes won't get them first.

That evening, after the kids went to bed, she heard the foxes howling out beyond the fence but she didn't turn on the porch light. They needed to be more discreet.

"Well done, love. For not feeding. It will get easier. They'll get used to it. They'll stop coming." Konrad was suddenly looking at her in a new way—or maybe he was getting that proud father-of-three look.

"Let's go to bed. I'm feeling better," she said.

He stood behind her, his one hand covering her entire stomach. Outside, a fox howled gently, with pleasure. Was it mummy fox, or daddy fox, she wondered. She took Konrad's hand: kissing one hard finger after another, counting to ten.

Permission to Bow

Like all great Polish writers, Jakub lives in the South of France, in a villa, drinking Chardonnay and speaking French to his wife. In the morning, his wife brings him coffee, says a polite *bonjour*, and bows. Jakub keeps on writing. He doesn't notice the coffee until it gets cold.

Jakub doesn't suffer from writer's block or blocks of any kind. It's because writing for him is pleasure, like sex with his French wife. He can't get enough of it. Sometimes Jakub writes before this pleasure or after. Sometimes he writes right in the middle of this pleasure. In fact, his best ideas come while enjoying his wife, and typing. They have a lot of special pleasure together. Often, his wife initiates it. She comes to his room and says *hey-hey*. She bows. She unzips his trousers. Often, he doesn't notice what she's doing until it's almost too late.

"Shall I continue?" asks his wife.

He starts typing faster and faster and she doesn't stop. Often, his best sentences are created that way.

Jakub writes many great short stories that way, too, and many novels. He suspects all great Polish writers living in the South of France do the same thing but they just don't tell anyone how they achieve their success.

Like many great Polish writers living in the South of France, Jakub is now very happy though he wasn't always happy in the past. This French wife is his second wife. His first wife was French, too, but she refused to tiptoe around him and pleasure him while he wrote.

"Did your wife like to make love—to you—while pregnant?" his second wife often asks about his first wife.

"No, she didn't," he says. It makes him sad. A little sad. He doesn't know why, exactly.

Then he thinks about his first wife again. She didn't make love to him then, no, not very much. Not when pregnant. She didn't like to be touched, maybe. Her beautiful body was pregnant with babies but she didn't want to share the pleasure of having them inside her, like a little secret, or an untold story. Not that pleasuring was ever important to Jakub. He just wrote. He wrote when his first wife loved him, and he wrote when she stopped.

His second wife was married before, too. This is her second try, a more successful match, Jakub hopes. A match from heaven, through hell, it feels like, to him, every day. This is due to the fact that Jakub is now a wise man and he knows how to please his wife—he knows her so well, it seems. He is now able to rewrite her past for her own advantage, or this is what he is trying to do, to make this marriage work.

"Tell me a secret, another secret, or the same one you told me about yesterday, but again," he asks his wife, every day.

"I am trying to remember," she tells him. "I have to think about it. I need time to think."

"Take your time," he says, but he can't wait, he just can't wait. He likes when his wife talks. He just closes his eyes and listens to her. She is full of secrets. There are things about her he doesn't understand. And when she talks, he asks her: Why? He asks it a lot.

For a start, why does she bow? It does feel strange sometimes, her bowing so much to him. Though Jakub is Polish and his wife is French, he lets her bow. It feels as if he allowed it. It feels, actually, as if she had asked. He gives her this permission—he thinks it's a permission—because he knows her darkest secrets, but not all of them. He is beginning to find out about her secrets, more and more. He is hoping that the more he learns about his wife, the more he can help her to be happy. Because the past will not just disappear, he is realising this now. He can't just delete it like a bad sentence; burn a bad novel. It doesn't work like that.

Like many great Polish writers living in the South of France, in a villa, drinking Chardonnay and speaking French to his wife; a wife that bows, continuously; bows in French; bows dressed; bows naked; bows with coffee and without, Jakub often asks his wife about her past, and why her first marriage broke down. Instead, she tells him about her five older brothers and what it was like to be locked in with them for five days, in a room, while their parents observed them through a little keyhole, in the French countryside, somewhere in Normandy, a long time ago. Jakub loves this story, as any great Polish writer would, of course, and he likes being told and re-told this story by his second French wife.

"This is not a story of abuse per se but rather great love and experimentation, and life really," he tells his wife.

"Yes," says his wife. "Things happen, in life." She nods. Or is it a little bow?

"Your parents of course were not nice," says Jakub. "They were simple, very cruel, and rather crude French farmers. But you coped. You found pleasure."

"I never thought of it like that," says his second wife.

Jakub asks about this story every day and he is rewriting the beginning every day, too. It's the most difficult story he has ever written, he thinks. It's because he is worried how he should tell it to his wife. This is a good story, he is thinking, and it sometimes goes like this: Jakub's second French wife is locked in with her five brothers, for five long days, at the sweet age of sixteen and of course she ends up bowing to them. But why? Why did this happen, in real life? Maybe she was stronger than her brothers. Maybe. Maybe not. Maybe she also coped much better with being locked in the same room. Maybe not. Maybe her five brothers just needed her support—or just something to do—while they waited for the doors to open. Maybe not.

When Jakub asks his wife what her brothers asked her to do, she tells him a different story every time. Sometimes she just talks about one of the brothers kissing her on the lips while the rest watched, waiting for their turn. Other times, she says she wasn't kissed on the lips but somewhere else.

"But where? Where did they kiss you?"

As a response, she only smiles, or cries. But smiles more often than she cries. Few tears, no sobs. Often, she talks about the kisses leading to something else, which she can't remember, not that day. She does, however, remember her parents taking her to the local abortion clinic. There are days when she says this happened much later, and not that very day, month, year.

When his wife tells him the story, Jakub tries not to imagine the parents looking through the keyhole, though he sometimes can't help thinking that by asking his wife to retell this story again and again—by obsessing about it so much—he is now looking at her though a little keyhole and imagining her as a sweet sixteen-year-old girl, and bowing to her brothers, and whatever happened next. Sometimes Jakub sees himself as her brother, and he is so gentle to her. Sometimes he is another brother, not so gentle.

Like all great Polish writers living in the South of France and drinking good wine with their good French wives, who bow and bow, Jakub thinks his wife might be deceiving him. He is worried that when she says she is meeting her friends in Paris, every spring, around Eastertime, she in fact goes to visit her brothers in a little village in Normandy, again and again. Her parents are there too, now very elderly but still cruel and controlling. They lock her in the same room for a few days and watch their six children—now adults in their forties—through the little keyhole maybe, again and again. They are so old they can't see much but they can hear something, surely.

Like all great Polish writers living in the South of France with a wife who is such a great mystery, like a book he is reading and reading, Jakub realises—more and more often—that he doesn't understand why his wife needs his permission to bow, and doesn't just bow if she wants to. He often wonders if it has anything to do with her thinking that bowing is inappropriate. In fact, maybe her bowing is something unnatural to her. Does she not feel adequate? After all, men and women are equal and they don't need to bow, not really.

Every time Jakub thinks of bowing, just bowing, anyone bowing—not just his wife—he realises this is not something he remembers from his childhood. Bowing was not how women behaved around him. His sisters didn't bow. His parents didn't bow. Nobody bowed. Bowing was not part of his upbringing. Women he knew were not always strong but neither did they bow. Even weak, frail, dying old women refused to bow. Even dogs didn't bow. Trees didn't bow. Nobody bowed.

He doesn't understand why his wife asks him for permission. Why every time she wants to bow, she asks: May I? She then bows so low that her nose almost touches the floor. In fact, sometimes her nose does touch the floor. If not the floor, then the zip of his trousers.

Like all great Polish writers living in the South of France with a wife who bows, just bows, and does it so beautifully that it is almost painful, Jakub realises—more and more often—that he doesn't know if he can or can't live without his wife, and her bowing. If his wife left him today, or tomorrow, would his writing suffer, or not at all? Would he get very depressed and commit suicide, or would he not? More importantly, would he write? Write better? Not write at all?

Jakub doesn't want his wife to go, of course. Nor does he want to be depressed or to commit suicide. But he is curious. If—one day—he didn't give his wife permission to bow, how would it affect his writing, and her?

So one day he tells her not to bow. In fact, he prohibits bowing.

At first, she doesn't obey. She keeps on bowing.

"Don't bow. I just want to see what happens if you don't bow. I just want to understand why bowing is so important to you; to me."

"*Non*," she says. "Never. Because I love you so."

Day after day, he begs her to stop bowing, until one day he dares her:

"Stop bowing, if you love me. Just for a day. One day. Please."

"So it's just a test?" She trusts him, it seems, day after day, more and more, but still she bows. So maybe she doesn't trust him. Not completely.

Then one day she says: "I want to stop, for you, but only because I am realising that ceasing all my bowing is in itself a sign of bowing. Not bowing is bowing more; and deeper, with more affection."

"Do you know how great you are?" he asks his wife. He asks her this question a lot. She just bows and says a quiet "thank you."

When she finally stops, which is both great and strange, it doesn't seem to affect his writing at all. Like all great Polish writers living in the South of France with a wife who bows, or doesn't bow, Jakub just keeps on writing, better than before, or perhaps just as well. There is no change. His wife, however, seems a little lost. Then—very unhappy. In fact, she looks more and more unhappy every day. So unhappy that Jakub is worried about her, more and more.

"What is the matter, my love?" He asks her, day after day.

She bursts into tears, every time he asks.

Slowly, she is beginning to talk. A little. A little every day, he hopes. Maybe more. Soon more.

She is remembering her childhood, she says, and her bowing *with* her brothers; *to* her brothers; *for* her brothers. Jakub asks her to tell him the exact story, every day, but she refuses. Every day, she remembers more and more, she says, but she seems to be saying less and less.

"Please," she asks him, again and again. "Just let me bow to you. Let me bow. I can't tell you. But I can show you maybe."

Like all great Polish writers living in the South of France, Jakub now permits bowing because the lack of it seemed to be killing his wife. He is now aware—more and more aware, every day—of the simple fact that his wife bows to him like she bowed before. It doesn't affect his writing—he can still write with or without his wife's bowing—but it affects what he is writing about. Not how though. Or why. Well, maybe a little.

At night, when he stops writing, he often reads his work to his wife. Or he is beginning to.

The story often describes two great Polish writers. The first writer in the story is a writer who has a lot of new ideas, a new idea every minute but can't carry on with any of them. Before he settles into one idea, another, better idea comes to his head and he gets distracted. The second writer has many good ideas too, but not as often. He is a bit slower than the first writer. But he can see logic between the ideas of the first great writer. Sometimes the logic is about removing one idea, somewhere in the story, and the story suddenly becomes great. The first writer is grateful for this, and bows.

"I didn't see how this idea is unnecessary," he says to the second great Polish writer. "But I still can't delete it. I find it hard to delete."

"Maybe don't delete it but use it in another story," says the second great writer. The first great Polish writer then bows to the second great Polish writer, thanking him for removing something from his story, or inserting it into another.

"Do you know how great you are?" The first great Polish writer asks the second great Polish writer, and really means it.

Jakub reads this story to his wife before bed. Every night, he then places his wife on top of five soft pillows and bows to her. The wife asks him to stop this, every night. She gets angry. She tells him that if he doesn't stop, she will kill herself, and him, every night. Often, she leaves the bedroom, slamming the doors.

Again, Jakub doesn't want his wife to go, or be depressed or commit suicide, or kill him, or slam the doors. So he is now working on another story. It's still a story of his wife bowing to her brothers though he is rewriting it from his earlier versions. Slowly, the story is beginning to say this: A whore, a great powerful whore, is born in the French countryside. She seduces her five older brothers, and even her elderly parents. She uses sex as a powerful tool to get what she wants: attention from parents, and love from her brothers. Nobody can resist her. Not even animals, or insects. Everybody loves her, everybody wants her. Jakub reads this story to his wife before bed. After, he places his wife on top of the five pillows, and again, as every night, he tries to bow. He even asks her permission now:

"Can I bow, please?"

"You know what I am going to say," says his wife, every day, but with less and less conviction maybe. Is she not sure?

Lately, he is beginning to bow to her, a little, just a little, with his head, like an almost imperceptible nod. And she is beginning to like it a little, it seems, a little more. She even smiles a little now. A little more than the night before. More and more. Little by little.

Oh My Gosh

—Why don't you write a story where a pussy is like a penis, in a society, you know, like it's very powerful?

—You mean now?

—Yes, *now*.

—But I can't think now. All I can say now is blah-bee blah blah.

—I love when you say blah-bee blah blah. You always say that when you are thinking with your pussy.

—That was nice. What you just did?

—I didn't do much. It doesn't need much.

—But you sort of pressed it, in the right place. Oh, I could just do nothing now. Nothing until you stop.

—Just write a little, OK? In this relaxed state.

—I can't type with my eyes closed, and when you press.

—You could dictate. Why don't you do that?

—I don't want you to stop doing what you are doing.

—I'll just record you, on my phone. I can type it for you later.

—All right. Fine.

—I'm ready. It's on. Go!

—My thighs are still hurting from last night but it's a nice pain.

—Is that how your story starts? I like this beginning.

—No, I was just saying that my thighs are still hurting, from last night. Blah-bee blah blah.

—Maybe if you open them just a bit more it will help?

—No, it's perfect as it is. Just continue, please. I like what you're doing. It's nice.

—Okay, but I'm really not doing much. Once you are in your story-telling mode, you become so animated and relaxed at the same time that you don't really need me very much. I become a facilitator. A coordinator for your stories. Not too hard?

—No, you could press a bit harder, actually.

—Like that?

—Yes. Funny, how men never know what to do with this spot. They sort of treat it like it's a penis, or an ear, or a breast.

—Men? Like your ex-husband?

—No, not just him. All men I have ever dated.

—Will you tell me about them?

—First, I half-dated my three half-brothers. We experimented, like children do. I guess these weren't dates but introductions to dates. I learned a lot from them.

—Like what?

—I just learned about men. What they like. How fragile they are.

—Yes, men are very fragile. Once, in primary school I was told off by my teacher for my messy handwriting. I still think this now. I'm this guy with very messy handwriting. This criticism, any criticism sticks to me always because I am imperfect somehow. Imperfection predates criticism. I'm not a woman with nice handwriting.

—This is what happened to one of my half-brothers too. He was told his reading wasn't fluent enough when he was seven and he still reads like a five-year-old at forty-four…

—But what about your story? About the hurting thighs?

—My thighs are still hurting from last night but they feel beautiful; they open and close.

—That's nice. I like that story. And who did you date after your half-brother? And what did you learn?

—I learned the most when I was pregnant. I lost all inhibitions and it was nice; things happened quickly. Once, I fussed so much I ended up in the hospital, with a bleed, but then they told me I was giving birth. So I don't know. Maybe I wasn't fussing too much. Maybe I was just giving birth.

—I like when you tell me this. When you say: I fussed. Can you put this in your thigh story? It tells me so much about you. You, you, you.

—Her thighs are still hurting from last night but they feel beautiful and she wants to fuss. The thighs open and close. He wants to make her pregnant. You're not jealous when I tell you about other men?

—No, I just see you, as the heroine. I am learning about what you like. But there is something wrong with the point of view in your story. First, you talk about the thighs hurting her, and then it's suddenly his point of view.

—He wants to make her pregnant.

—Are we now in his head? So he sees her, and her beautiful thighs… So beautiful. But you said that you like being pregnant?

—Yes, I think it's my favourite state. I wish I was pregnant still. Maybe we could pretend? And fuss, like I'm pregnant?

—I think once you gave birth you *are* always pregnant. You became Gosh.

—I'm Gosh? Oh my Gosh. Wait, I need to scream now.

—I like your animal noises.

—Animal? I thought you said I was Gosh?

—Well, yes, you are Gosh. But when I said it to you, you replied: 'Oh my Gosh.' Just flagging this for you. It's pretty good. Could go in your story maybe?

—But when I said 'oh my Gosh' I actually imagined a man, you know, not a woman. A bearded man. Wait, I'm going to scream again. Push harder, now.

—Oh, I like these Gosh noises.

—Men's noises?

—No, I said Gosh's.

—Men's. I heard men's.

—Gosh's. Jesus, just accept you are Gosh. Gosh, Gosh, Gosh. You are Gosh. Not me. You. You are *Gosh*. You and your thighs.

—What makes you so sure?

—Well, the very fact we all imagine Gosh as a man just proves that he is definitely not a man. But tell me your story. The thighs story. So you experimented with your brothers, then went on various dates with men who believed your clitoris was a third ear, then you got pregnant, then you gave birth, and now you are a mother, with a lover, and your thighs are hurting.

—Yes, then I became a mother, and then a lover.

—Gosh.

—No, a mother and lover.

—Well, but isn't every mother-lover like Gosh really?

—I guess. It felt very powerful. Motherhood. This almost-nine-month production of life. It was a powerful process. And so was the birth. My birth. It was my birth, too. It woke me up to many things, to life, to real life. To feeling. Blah-bee blah blah.

—It made you Gosh.

—Well, yes, I felt a bit like Gosh after. I gave birth and then I had a shower.

—You could walk?

—Yes, it was easy. Painful but ecstatic. My thighs hurt then too, in a different way.

—Now, I feel jealous. A little.

—Jealous of what?

—Just that pain and ecstasy I will never experience, as a man. Even the thighs. The pain in your thighs.

—So you think fatherhood is different?

—Fatherhood is about realising you are powerless. Your child is born and you become a spare wheel. A provider. A carer for your family. You put together the crib. You put together the high chair. You drive to the store for milk, nappies…

—Light bulbs?

—Light bulbs and so forth. You are the last on the list, with the least number of wants, needs, desires.

—That's sad. I'm sorry.

—Fatherhood is grief, you know. Fatherhood is death.

—No, it can't be. Not always. Tell me more. But please, don't stop pressing, OK?

—Sorry, my finger got cramped. Well, that's why men invented the story of Gosh. Gosh being a man. To make them feel a bit better about themselves. Even if I am the least important person in my family, I represent Gosh, you see. I look like Gosh. I am powerful. I have a beard—or I can, if I want.

—Oh, so it's a story men tell themselves? And they tell it to women? And their children?

—We tell it to everyone, and everyone believes us. But it's a big fat lie.

—Yes, I've heard this story so many times I want to believe in it. It's been programmed into me, and I find comfort in it, just as I find comfort in you pressing now, with your finger. Is your finger better?

—I swapped fingers. I was using my index finger before, and now I am just using the little finger, just pressing very gently. In fact, maybe you could use your own finger and press, and as soon as you do, you will see how little I'm doing, and then you'll know the story is a lie! You will discover you don't need me, for anything other than a little seed, or two. Or to make your thighs hurt a little.

—I know it's a lie but without this story, I no longer find you attractive, somehow. I don't want to be more powerful than you.

Well, maybe sometimes. I can be the boss. Sometimes I am a little bossy. Try a thumb now! Then try your index finger again! Now! Make my thighs hurt!

—You *are* bossy. Gosh, you are. That's why a female scorpion, I think, just kills the father when the little scorpions are born. He served his purpose, you see, and she no longer needs him. He becomes a nuisance.

—I feel sorry for daddy scorpion. Can't he stay? Maybe the car could use a wash. Maybe the satellite dish needs adjusting. Why don't you stop pressing and just come here? I want to give you a hug.

—You've had enough? Was it boring? Tell me, was I not paying attention?

—No, I want you to hug me. I want to feel like a woman held by Gosh, you know, the way I imagine Gosh. I want to kiss your hand and fingers. I want to worship you, like Gosh.

—Just don't call me Gosh, OK? I hate that male Gosh, with the big long Santa beard, jeez.

—But can I worship you, please, like a woman in love? Even though for generations and generations, since caveman times perhaps, since forever, you lied to me about Gosh?

—I lied to you, and you want me to lie more? Like I made your thighs hurt and you want me to hurt you more? To keep on lying; hurting? What do you feel when you worship then? Does it feel nice?

—I feel a certain kind of pleasure but only if you worship me too. No, it's not worship. I don't want to be worshiped, as a woman.

—Just let me press one more time, with the longest finger I have.

—That's nice, like super nice. Which finger was that again? I think we should label all your fingers, they all feel a little different, you know.

—I don't need labels. I've been paying attention. I've been observing you. I know what each finger does. You even tilt your head in a different way, with each finger.

—Gosh. That's so nice what you just said. About attention. Paying attention. I think I just want to be admired.

—Admired? That's all? You don't want any power? You just want me to see you? With thighs like that you could rule the world.

—Yes, I just want to be noticed, by you. That's all. I don't ever want to become invisible to you. This would kill me.

—I would never do that. Let you become invisible. I couldn't.

—Let me tell you a story. A parable. There was once a penis and a pussy in the Sahara. The penis was hard and big, a bit like a cock. You know, a little arrogant. So he said to the pussy: "You are just a cave. I am better than you." And then the moment he said it, the sandstorm began, and the cock quickly hid inside the pussy.

—Hid? Is that what you think he was doing? Maybe he was exploring. Like an explorer, like Indiana Jones, looking for treasure.

—No, I'm pretty sure he hid. The cock was very afraid.

—Did the pussy let him, after he offended her?

—Well, yes, she did because when he was about to enter her, he said: "Oh, Gosh, I didn't quite realise how beautiful you are. So beautiful."

—Ah, see, the magic words. Open sesame, etc.

—Don't you think that's what Gosh wants, for us to see him? I mean, *her*. Isn't that all? Just observe? Pay attention? See? Just see?

—Yes, and feel maybe, like I feel you, in my arms. You feel warm, and sweet, just sweet, so open now, are ready, just ready for anything, and I could just always hug you like this. I don't even want to fuss with you. I just want to hug you. Just hug, OK? And look at your thighs.

—But what if *I* want to fuss with you? Just fuss, for Gosh's sake, fuss, with no hugs? Enough of hugs now! I want to fuss. A little. I want to fuss hard.

—OK, just don't rush, OK? Let me admire you more. Everything, even your smell. Yes, you have a smell. It's not bad. Is it sweetness, or just you? Your smell, sweet but also just full of loveliness. What Gosh smells like maybe? Can I worship you, just a little, just a tiny little bit, please?

—No, not now, it will spoil everything. I don't want to be bossy now. I feel weak, and I just want to be picked up and carried to bed and kissed. I want to show you my weak side, my worshipping side. I want you to be bossy with me, a little, just carry me to bed rather than ask if you even can. I mean, you know I want it, because I just told you, so just wait a bit and pay attention, and then boss me a little, tell me more lies, tell me that you are Gosh, and that I should worship you, and I'll believe your lies, and worship you, until I am in a bossy mood again and I suddenly want all your attention, all at once, immediately, which you could confuse for worship, but it's not worship. It's just admiration.

—But you are bossy, like all the time. Jeez. Even if you tell me that I should be a little bossy, you are still saying this in a bossy way. Like a bossy woman. You're a total bossy boots, Gosh. What are you doing?

—I'm fussing with you.

—Yes, I can tell. But did you ask?

—No! I helped myself. Because, oh my Gosh, I just believed you. It's my new story: I am Gosh. I believed you, like totally. Entirely. You were right. You were right. Twice. No, three times. Every time, in fact. Every time, I will believe you. Now, now, and now. And with my thighs.

Ka-boom

Like all great writers and mothers of two, Mummy lives in south-east London, in a villa, drinking bubbly wine and speaking English. In the morning, Daddy brings her tea with a slice of lemon, says a polite "good morning, darling," and bows. Mummy keeps on writing. She doesn't seem to notice the tea until it gets cold.

"Is this some kind of lemonade?" she often asks Daddy half an hour later when she finally sips her tea. Daddy then says, "Sorry," and removes the cold tea from the table, bowing again.

"Dorothea, can you make me a proper cuppa, for goodness' sake?" she then asks, although she sometimes says "for fuck's sake" if she is very thirsty.

Dorothea makes her a proper cuppa. The trick to a proper tea with lemon is to serve it with a special glass straw, and to stay with

Mummy until the tea becomes just the right temperature to drink it, not too cold and not too hot, and to remind her every now and again to drink it while she writes, and to bow every time she sips.

After her tea, Mummy, Leonard, and Dorothea put their bulletproof vests on and go shopping to Harrods where Mummy meets Pepe, her publicist, for a coffee and sometimes for lunch. Harrods is a nice shop with a lot of security and CCTVs. At Harrods, Mummy buys Dorothea a new Barbie and a pink dress made by Victoria's Secret for Kids, every day, and a new toy Ferrari for little Leonard and sometimes a new pair of Gucci jeans for him, too.

Mummy and Pepe discuss things at Harrods. Not just books but life too. They sometimes say "Ka-boom!" to each other, and out of the blue. Sometimes "Ka-boom!" is why Mummy writes maybe, Pepe says. Often, there is a text message that Pepe gets about a successful ka-boom somewhere. Very successful, he says, and Mummy claps her hands, and then she makes notes for her next short story, poem, play, or novel. Just quick notes which say "ka-boom" often, in every line. Ka-boom this, ka-boom that.

At Harrods, Mummy often buys furniture, lipstick, iPhones, and of course iPhone covers. Mummy often loses her phones, or changes her mobile number, or says her iPhone exploded in her hand. At Harrods, she gets discounts. For example with every new iPhone, she gets a new iPhone cover with "Ka-boom!" written on it, with Swarovski's crystals. Often, with each new iPhone cover, "Ka-boom!" gets bolder, bigger, and shinier, with even more crystals.

Little Leonard and Dorothea don't go to school with other children. Instead, Elena, Dorothea's private tutor, always comes with them to Harrods. This is how Dorothea learns new things, every day: From ten till one-thirty in the afternoon, Elena and Dorothea count all dresses on each floor, and then discuss their style, and try to think of a period in history when the dress, or certain style, was popular, for example: collapsed sleeves, low necklines, or elongated V-shaped bodices. They talk about the history and geography; of where the dresses, and their fabrics, come from. They calculate how much they would cost if they were twenty, thirty, and fifty percent off. They discuss how much it really costs to make and ship the dress from overseas, and how much it costs at Harrods. They change currency from pound to dollar and then to Australian dollar, Canadian dollar, Yuan Renminbi, złoty, dirham, or the Euro. They also sometimes discuss Victorian times, if they are at Victoria's Secret for Kids and Queen Victoria's reign, and ladies who wore these lovely dresses but who could not vote, no matter how pretty they looked, or how rich they were. Then Elena tells Dorothea about the history of colonisation, country by country, the world falling apart as a result. But not for long, Elena says. Soon things might improve a little, she always says. Dorothea often doesn't know what Elena means exactly when she says this, she doesn't see how things could be even better for them, but she guesses Elena is working on some plan, with a lot of other people, and Mummy too, or she knows the future maybe, and the future is so bright, it seems. She is a teacher after all, so she knows, surely. Mummy knows everything, too.

Mummy often shows Dorothea and Leonard her latest book covers. They'll be sitting at Harrods' cafe in the afternoon, just enjoying champagne for kids and caviar. Mummy's covers often have sweets on them, or foxes, which are Dorothea's favourite animals. Sometimes they have trees, and rivers, and mountains, and little explosions.

"What do you think, Dorothea?" Mummy asks.

"Not enough pink," Dorothea says. "I want more pink in that fire over London, please, Mummy. Not just red and purple flames, OK? Pink flames too, please. And lots of them."

Mummy tilts her head and squints her eyes, as if she was trying to see the cover again and again. Often she gets a text message. If she does, she claps her hands.

"Yes, Pepe, more pink for the fourth edition, please," says Mummy, in a happy voice.

"And the fifth? Can I decide about the fifth?" asks little Leonard.

Mummy strokes and kisses Leonard's head. She often does it to him, no matter what he says. She often does it even if he is a bit naughty.

"Of course. What do you think, children? More animals on the cover? More trees?" she asks them about another cover.

"I want more sweets," says Leonard.

"You mean on the cover?" asks Mummy. "Between the trees? Or in the sky? Next to the sun? Sweets instead of clouds?"

"Yes. And in life. I want life to be sweet, Mummy. Always sweet, like now."

"Oh, that's nice," says Mummy.

"Shall I buy Leonard more sweets?" asks Pepe.

"No, that's fine. My personal assistant can do that," says Mummy, because they often have Mummy's personal assistant with them when we go to Harrods. He is a nice Swedish man called Emil. Daddy used to be the assistant but Mummy said he wasn't very good and kept forgetting about things, like tea, or getting angry, or wasn't a good team member or said bad things about "Ka-booms," which upset Mummy, so now Daddy stays at home making little models of German tanks while Emil—who is more organised—comes with them instead.

When Dorothea looks at Mummy's book covers, she realises that Mummy's book covers up until now have always been very pink, always pink. But recently Dorothea's favourite colour became green. It's just a nice colour. It's not the regular grass green that she likes the most; more like minty green. That's why Mummy's covers are now turning minty, too. It's Dorothea's influence.

"Can we have more mint?" Dorothea tells Pepe, because she no longer likes pink very much, she doesn't think. She hates pink now, more and more, she is almost ten after all, so even when there are explosions on Mummy's book covers, could they not have explosion in the colour of mints? She asks this question a lot lately.

"We can certainly have more minty green everywhere," says Pepe.

"Can we have more foxes?" asks Leonard.

"Yes, we can have more foxes if Leonard would like it that way," Pepe says to Mummy, and Leonard too, as if foxes were a colour, and maybe they are a colour, a foxy colour. Sometimes Leonard says it about trees, if there is only one tree on the cover and Leonard happens to want more trees, three for example. "Yes, let's make it three," says Pepe, every time.

Leonard often just hangs off the chair, with his legs sticking up in the air. "Can we have an explosion on the cover?" he says. "Or three trees, and three explosions, and three Suns, three rivers, and three bowing men, all exploding?" Leonard is currently obsessed with the number three, it seems. For him, everything needs to come in threes or it's imperfect maybe. Or maybe it's because he is three now, so he wants to understand what being three really means, surely.

"What's three times three hundred and thirty-three?" asks Elena, and Dorothea can never remember, so she ignores her question for a minute or two. Or three.

"Ka-boom," says Pepe. He says it a lot, every hour lately, looking at his phone and then Dorothea remembers the answer. It's nine hundred and ninety-nine, of course. Always.

Every day, when they get back from Harrods, Mummy writes in the evenings, too, in her bed but still with her vest on. She writes books, as if she already had them in her head; she writes quickly, as if someone were holding a gun to her head. Mummy just likes writing, Dorothea guesses. Mummy likes to write with her two fingers only, her index fingers, and sometimes her middle fingers. But she does it very quickly, so it doesn't look like she can't type. But it does look like she is rushing. Maybe there is an invisible gun against her head that only she can see?

Daddy often tries to serve Mummy a hot glass of milk around this time. He comes to the bedroom and bows.

"Yes?" asks Mummy, every time. She doesn't stop typing.

Daddy leaves the hot milk on her side table. Mummy doesn't notice the milk until it gets cold.

"Dorothea, can I have some hot milk, for goodness' sake," she asks half an hour later, when she finally sips her now-cold milk.

The trick to getting Mummy to drink her hot milk is exactly the same as the trick with hot tea and lemon: to serve it with a special glass straw and stay with her until the milk becomes just the right temperature to drink it, not too cold and not too hot, and then remind her every now and again to drink it while she writes, and bow every time she sips.

This way, because Mummy writes all the time, she at least drinks a little, if she forgets to eat. She has a new book coming out every season, so she is busy. One for spring, one for autumn and one for winter. Mummy never writes in the summer though. Every summer, Mummy, Leonard, and Dorothea travel places with Emil, wearing their bulletproof vests, and then Mummy just enjoys life, drinking cups of teas with lemon, every hour. Where they choose to go is totally accidental but they always stay in five-star hotels. They often just close their eyes and pick a place on the globe, and then they go there, with lots of iPhones. Mummy says iPhones are the new currency. But she also says iPhones are imperfect and they often explode, so they need some spare ones. Even if they are on holidays and just having a nice time, there are always explosions wherever they go. Not in their hotel, but in the hotel next to theirs. Nobody knows who does it, and then—after the explosion happens—the manager of the hotel sends some money to a poor country, and starts supporting a little poor village somewhere, or a poor family, or a poor child, and it seems to be linked to the explosion maybe, but who knows.

Mummy writes the most before Christmas. She is so busy she stops eating and drinking completely. The straw in her tea has reindeer on it. Harrods is beautiful then and full of Christmas trees and decorations and Swarovski's crystals everywhere. But Mummy seems to pay no attention to all this. She just writes. Dorothea often just stares at Mummy, stares and stares, thinking how great their life is, how happy clappy, among all these sparkly things, and how for them, it's Christmas every single day really, whether Mummy eats or forgets to eat. Mummy writes, and it makes everyone so very happy.

The Christmas Pig

It was Christmas, which should've made it easier to do the killing. A special occasion. But it wasn't just a regular pink pig. It had a name. Dracula. Poor Dracula, Katie thought. Before the war, it could roam the streets of Hollywood, USA, with other pigs and chickens. Now, it had to be locked up in a small wooden crate, like a prisoner.

Katie stroked his ears. Dracula's tail wagged like a dog's. Such a young, happy dog-pig.

"Are you still hungry, Dracula? Want some more semolina?"

"Oink, oink," said Dracula.

"Shhhh," she said. Don't make so much noise or they will find you. "Sit!"

Dracula sat, like a dog.

He is getting fatter day by day, Katie thought. So lazy. Growing meat. Growing a good sausage under his skin. But he is getting louder, with the oinking. Louder and louder. It's dangerous.

Her children went to bed hungry today, with no meat in their tummies. How strange that she felt no guilt. Her children were strong—like her. Unbreakable. And Manolo? Why him, and not somebody else, last night? He was somebody to talk to, really. A gentleman, with large gentle hands. And no shame, not in war-time, not in the last days of this stupid summer, two-thousand and forty-one. And money, she needed money. To feed the pig so that she could usually, in theory, feed the children. She had to feed them. They had to eat every other day at least.

The pig's ears felt soft to touch.

"Somebody will have to cut your throat, Dracula." She made a sign of the cross on pig's chest. "Who is it going to be—now that they have taken Father away? It won't be Jeremy."

She waved to Dracula, as if to say good-bye, and closed the doors of the pig house behind her, locking it twice. Several steps through the garden, and she was back on the porch. A few steps up again, and she was in bed, Jeremy already there: his nose in his book, sitting on the bedspread rather than covered with it. *The Book of the Thousand Nights and a Night.*

"How do Arabs kill pigs, Jeremy?" she asked and sat down next to him on the bedspread. He always wore socks in bed. And long johns underneath his pajama bottoms.

"I don't know. Why?"

"I imagined I was a beautiful Arab princess."

"You are American, and very boring, I'm afraid. But a princess nonetheless." He yawned loudly.

"How does the Russian aristocracy kill old dogs then?"

"Are you now a Russian princess?"

"Suppose I am."

"They don't. They let them die by natural causes. And then they eat the old dog."

"I'm serious, Jeremy."

"I'm serious too when I tell you I don't know. Can I read my book?"

"You never talk to me anymore. You treat me as if I was your child." She felt tears, so she quickly exhaled lots of air. It always helped. Just exhaling all the toxins. Tears were toxins, too, mixed with water. It was good to cry, just not next to him. Never.

"It's because you are never home when I want to talk to you."

"I'm home now."

"But I'm out." He snapped his fingers, like a magician demonstrating a "snap vanish" card trick.

"Jeremy, please. Think of something sad for a minute."

"I don't have to think hard to think of sad things." He said it very slowly rather than sadly.

"Why? What makes you sad? The saddest?"

"When I think of Dracula dying." He didn't look sad.

"He is growing fast, Jeremy. He is ready to die. You don't want a pig the size of a cow, do you? The meat won't be as tender."

Jeremy put the book away on the side table. He took her hand and kissed her knuckles, one by one. He kicked off the bedspread. Her face now against the pillow rather than the wall, no beard scratching the back of her neck but the same hands, it seemed, holding her breasts tight. "You are so sweet now," he said. Then he came. Wasn't it exactly what Manolo said, and did, earlier, and at the same moment? Manolo at least paid her. Paid her for her sweetness while her husband did not. Where was this sweetness born exactly, she wondered, and why was there so much of it? So good to think of Manolo. Manolo gave her strength to survive this. He gave her money. Money was important. Money freed them, made them honest to each other. Sometimes he gave her food. Sometimes she gave him blow jobs. They didn't play any games.

"So sweet, you are almost boring, Katie."

He picked up his book again, as if the book was better than her, better than reading her, her true nature. She asked him if it wasn't in fact good to be boring. "Or does that mean dull, to you, Jeremy?" she asked. Lovemaking was like flipping the page of his book maybe. So insignificant to him. Maybe if he had known she was a whore, he would have treated her better? A little better? But he was now happy in bed, reading. Reading about Arab princesses and whores. Maybe that was his way, with the war?

"Yes, it's what attracted me to you first. Your ability to open up your legs so wide." He found the middle of the book, and flapped the book's wings.

"And now you find it boring?"

"No, it's pure poetry. Most women need more time."

"And it bothers you?"

"Not at all. It just puzzles me, your readiness."

"But sometimes you're quite ready, too."

"I'm always ready when you are." He closed his book. "Good story."

"How do you know then that I'm ready?"

"You sort of always are, these days."

"Is that bad?"

"No, but it makes me think that you are becoming a middle-aged woman, Katie. No. Not Katie. I should call you Catherina."

"Well, we are not planning more children, are we?"

"Not that I know of."

"So why don't you want me to be ready for lovemaking, all the time?"

"I used to have to ask you twice. For everything. I asked you twice to come home with me, nine years ago. Then I asked you twice to marry me, even though you were already pregnant with twins."

"Did you like to ask twice?"

"I don't know, I don't think I did. But recently you've lost something."

"You are confusing me, Jeremy. You are a confused man."

"You don't make me wait anymore. You are no longer a girl, or something. You've become a woman maybe. I think this war—it sort of is—your thing. Your prime time. It opens you up."

"War is not my prime time."

"It makes you more beautiful. The more dangerous the world, the more you thrive." He was talking with his back turned to her now; away from her beauty.

"Why isn't it your prime time then?"

"I see too much suffering." He yawned again.

"Don't we all?" Yawning now would be like agreeing with what he was saying, so she resisted it with all the force she could find.

"I think there is a terrible thing happening."

"In Dickens? Flaubert."

"In real life, woman. Last Friday. In Washington, DC. Two thousand American Jews killed! In one day! They are now looking for the rest. Jason the baker. He's on their list. And his family. They will come for them this week. I saw the list, at work. You know him, don't you? We must help them!"

She was already helping Jason. Or he was helping himself, with all she had to offer to a man. He paid her well too. Not as much as Manolo, but he paid. "Two thousand is a lot," she said. And then: "Jesus, it's like Poland a hundred years ago. The Poland my granny told me about. Fucking America. Now invaded too."

"Someone told me that you are good friends." It sounded as if he had made special effort not to say: "History likes to repeat itself." But what did he know? He would never believe the sort of things she did for her children. That's what she always thought: it's for the children, their well-being: Jews, Mexicans, Poles, Jamaicans. As long as they paid.

"I'm good friends with everybody, Jeremy."

"You don't need to be good friends with other men."

"Are you jealous?"

He laughed, as if she said something funny. "Of course not. We'll take them in for a few days. Let them lie low. Confuse the authorities. Next, they can go and live with the neighbours. Then—we'll send them to the countryside."

"Is it necessary—for them to leave town?"

"Yes. And for Jason to shave off his beard."

In her house, she thought. Jason, and Rachel, and all their loud kids, playing with her loud kids. Ten mouths.

When Jeremy fell asleep, she went barefoot in her night dress through the dark garden, to see Dracula again, with a knife.

By the time Jason and his family arrived, dinner had been made. And not just any dinner. It was Dracula's shoulder roasting in the oven, with garlic and honey.

Rachel came in first, holding two girls—by their hands. Not as strong or tall as me, Katie thought, as if strength and height were the measurements of beauty. As if beauty was just vigour, in Katie's world. Less beautiful? Not at all, but less confident. Could she ever say to Jason, *Make love to me?* No, Katie didn't think so. Could she stand up to an entire army of men, confident, walking up to them, not scared? Maybe Katie could. But Rachel? No, she was too scared of men. If anyone tried to take away this delicious pig from their table now, only Katie could stand up to them; the soldiers, the baddies. It came down to one thing: politeness in bed. Was Rachel polite in bed? She was, yes, very polite, for sure. So polite in fact, that she dictated the entire act like a tyrant: so fragile, so easy to hurt, so difficult to please, just impossible to love.

Behind Rachel, Jason now stepped in, with a little bundle of their clothes, tied with a rope. Behind him was his son, holding a bunch of roses. If this was just a quick visit, for a Sunday roast, then the son and the flowers would have come first—and not last.

"Please," said Katie. "Come in, and make yourselves at home. Dinner's ready. Christmas dinner, in fact. Isn't it Christmas today?"

They moved about the house furtively, as if they were still on the street—Rachel still holding the girls by their hands—her long scarf still on. Jason and his son didn't remove their hats, or shoes. They sat by the table taking the first available seats: a family boarding a train.

Katie sat too, looking away, into the kitchen. She tried to imagine how and when things got complicated between Rachel and Jason. Was it when—like every month—Rachel was *niddah* and he had to wait? Wait! He! The man! For three long days! Sleeping in the spare, uncomfortable bed, or not even allowed to pass her a plate. Then, the mandatory seven days before she immersed herself in a *mikveh*, the ritual bath, which wasn't even that nice, or hot. Perhaps that's what killed their love, in the end. The waiting, and the hope that—each month—she would ovulate before, and not after, *mikveh*? Then him back in her bed; her monthly cycle right in the dangerous middle. Were there other secrets to Rachel and Jason's lovemaking she didn't know about, or was it like American and Jewish cuisine, all mixed up and inseparable, and so controlled by women, not men?

She looked at Rachel again: her body demanding respect, and care. No, it wasn't that. It wasn't about lovemaking; Rachel was lovable, but difficult. Maybe she just became difficult somewhere along the way. Not an easy woman, not as easy to be with as Katie.

"Here comes the roast." Jeremy hovered with his tray over the table.

"Pork?" asked Rachel when his knife drowned in the meat.

"Chicken," said Jeremy.

"No, the truth is—it *is* pork, Rachel." Katie stood up from her chair and poured the cooking juices over the roast, as if it was a magic potion that would change it into something else. "I'm sorry. It's all we had. But I can make you a fried egg. Or semolina."

"That's fine, I'm not hungry."

"You should eat something, Rachel," said Jason. It sounded as if he said it a lot, every day, at every mealtime. He then removed his hat and put it by his plate—a resignation.

Katie began serving the children first. Big chunks of meat, with potatoes mashed up with butter and finely chopped parsley—from the garden. They all ate, with their knives and forks. This always worked, Katie thought, feeding children together, in a large group. They never rejected food then, or misbehaved. Maybe they should always have people over for dinner? If she could, she would feed all the children she knew, the entire street! But then how often did they eat meat now? Once a month? The rest of the time it was semolina, or eggs.

Rachel began stroking her scarf, as if it was her hair. She was staring at her empty plate.

Jeremy said: "Are you sure, Rachel? I'm a terrible cook, but I tried so hard tonight."

"So you've made it? The entire roast?" Rachel opened her mouth and looked at Jeremy with admiration.

"My wife killed the pig and cooked it. I sprinkled the salt, and the pepper. So, it's a man's roast. Which doesn't mean it's just for kids, and men. Please, try a little. I'll ask you again and again—all night long if I have to."

"I'm sorry, Rachel. He is terrible," Katie tapped Jeremy on the shoulder, as if they were a happily married couple, joking around. "But shall I give you a little piece—a very little piece?" Katie put a small piece of pork on her serving spoon: "As small as a tooth, dear? Like that? Just to taste?"

"Here comes your chicken," said Jeremy, and he served Rachel some potatoes, splashing them on her plate.

"Don't start a food fight, dear," Katie said to him. Rachel laughed into her fist, coughing. She took off her scarf and hung it over the chair. Her neck like a young swan's. She had beautiful eyes. Dying eyes.

"You've got quite a joker there," Rachel said.

Katie looked at Jeremy. She wanted to shout at him, across the table. She is sick—with the war! So sick she cannot eat! Stop forcing the food. And yet, she placed a tiny cube of pork on her plate, too. She looked at Jason. Her dear Jason. Was it easier for him to just make love to Katie and pay her for it? Because she *could* eat?

Katie left an unfinished piece of pork on her plate, then collected the dishes from the table and took them into the kitchen. She wanted to cry but couldn't. Maybe later, she thought, alone. I'll go into the garden and have a little cry, in the night, in Dracula's empty shed.

She heard Rachel talking. "You are a very nice family," she said, presumably to Jeremy. "And I would like to say, come and see us soon too." The kids were having apple cake now—with no cinnamon, and no raisins, and no whipped cream—but still, apple cake, with Golden Delicious apples from her garden. She never saw children behave so well.

"Merry Christmas," said Katie.

We All Marry Our Mothers

Helena and Mother were standing in the kitchen, side by side, by the cooker.

"So you need to fight her, Helena," Mother said. "Be tough." Mother was back from the studio; still wearing black leather trousers, red stilettos, and a blue lace shirt. She stirred the tomatoes in the pan, tapping them with a wooden spoon, as if hurrying them to simmer more quickly, so that she could add water and make the soup, with some rice.

"Fight? But I'm better than that. I'm better than him. I'll ask him to leave," Helena said.

"You won't survive without a man. You'll get killed, or raped, or both. Especially in Hollywood." Mother took the reddest tomato out of the pan, lifted it with the spoon, smelled it, and then let it splash back. Of course, she just assumed that Helena had no men around her, no men other than her husband, but Helena was always surrounded by men. She was always one step away from an affair maybe. An affair which could progress if only Helena took it further but she didn't. Of course not. She was married, still married, and she had children, so why would she want to confuse the children and everybody else, especially now, with war everywhere? Wasn't the world—with this awful war—confusing enough?

"I want him to move out, Mother!"

"Move out? You are crazy!"

"I want to divorce him!"

"Did you not hear me? A woman can't survive without a man."

"Nonsense!" Helena closed her eyes and saw red again. Then purple. She imagined her complexion like the skin of the tomatoes in the pan, getting tighter and redder.

"A roll with butter it is not. But divorce, Helen? You can't divorce. Wait till the war ends. Pray. Talk to God. See a priest."

"A priest? But my husband is betraying me! Like an enemy!"

"Husbands usually do."

"Do they? Then I want justice. A good solicitor!"

"A solicitor? People have no food in this town, and you want justice? Even solicitors are dying of starvation. It's just an affair. It will pass. Another year or two or three and it will be over and done with. Like the war. It will pass, with the war."

"Three long years, Mother?"

"Maybe only six months."

"I want to see a solicitor."

"Wake up, Helena. This is not Turkey. This is not Syria. Or Egypt. This is America. The Western front, for God's sake. Most solicitors died—in the ghetto. And now they are killing the French!"

Helena thought of the Durands. They were perhaps the only French family left in town and still hiding, although Helena never thought of them as hiding or on the run. Or French. They had been coming for "sleepovers." For the past four years they had sleepovers in various friends' houses around Hollywood. Dinners, drinks, bridge, and then a quick bath, and more drinks. Then a night in the attic and their loud lovemaking.

Mother added water to the pan which immediately turned red, like blood.

"So who do I talk to, Mother?"

"Talk to his mother. She might help."

"His mother! I have nothing to say to his mother other than go to hell. And you, Mother, you are not helping either. Not even a little."

"Nonsense," said Mother. She was difficult, always so difficult, saying "no" where she could easily say "yes." It occurred to Helena that all men in her life somehow resembled Mother. David, for a start. He was grumpy and moody like her mother and distant like her too. Like her mother, he could not cope with being needed. He didn't know how to give anyone in despair any kind of hope. Not that Helena was ever in despair. She wasn't. She was always full of hope, or so she hoped.

Mother put the steaming soup on the dinner table. Oh, Mother cooked such lovely soups! And maybe this was the problem. Helena turned a blind eye to any bad news.

The cigarette in Mother's mouth made her look younger. Or maybe it was her very blue shirt? They were still sitting by the dinner table, now having coffee.

"The button," Mother said and took off her blue shirt. It had a blue button missing. Her eyes didn't change colour. Still bright blue. Blue, everywhere she looked.

The coffee smelled good despite just being chicory. It almost looked dark blue too. Navy blue. Mother stood up from the table.

"Can you sew this button on for me, Helena?"

Of course, Helena could sell buttons, if she had a shop. Heaps of buttons every day. But sewing them on? It was too domestic and required too much patience, and no spectators. Selling was a transaction, an exchange. It was exciting. It involved four eyes. Sewing didn't. It was just about a button, and a lonely pair of eyes. Three eyes, counting the button's.

So lonely. With no husband. Sewing. With Mother at the table like a director. With nobody. Nobody but Mother.

She got her sewing kit down from a cabinet. Red threads, yellow green, and blue. Now all one colour, really, to Helena. Sobbing began with the shoulders, then the knees which shook. Helena felt the knees move to the side, too, while the shoulders moved up and down. Then came salty tears in her throat. And then sudden anger at everything and everyone.

"Now, stop crying, Helena," said Mother. "Stop crying immediately. Men are not worth it. Just do some sewing. It will help. It will calm the nerves."

Calm the nerves? Here, I hate sewing. Here, I hate you, Mother.

The sound of a ripping shirt, ripping fast. One by one, she pulled all six buttons off her shirt. She imagined Mother's dark old brown nipples.

"I'm sorry," Mother quickly stood up from her chair, as if the house were on fire, just to pat Helena on the shoulder. "So sorry. Did it all just hit you? Your life. No future. Your marriage. I don't think I can help." She had blue tears in her blue eyes.

Help? She gulped for air, or maybe for her cigarette smoke— still in the air. Helena never smoked but now wanted to smoke, for the first time ever. Mother's warm hand on her neck now. Gentle strokes, as if she were a cat.

"What is it that you need, Helena?" she asked. "You know, I can't help, but maybe you want to talk?"

"I need to open up a shop, Mother." Her voice felt stronger than her shaking knees. She wanted to find work, spend less time at home. But what would change? For Helena change was always about reinstalling the old, really. Putting the old button back in its rightful place. Change was about not changing at all. Change was about staying Helena, despite the world moving on without her; despite her husband's new woman; despite Mother's games; and in spite of them.

"I'm sorry, Helena," Mother then said. "I'm sorry for causing you so much pain. But I thought it would be easier for you to just be busy. Busy with domestic stuff."

Helena was ready to kill, with her bare hands. Or with no hands, but eyes only.

"Let me go and do something else."

"But I have plans for you here. Big plans." Mother pointed at the kitchen.

"It will be autumn soon," Helena said.

"Autumn?"

"Everybody needs umbrellas—in the rain."

"You are thinking about *umbrellas*—now?"

"There are also scarves that I could sell, Mother."

The window, she wanted to be by the window. She opened it just enough to smell the rain and the air which felt moist in her throat and nostrils. Refreshing? Yes, a change of weather was always refreshing. It smelled of September, new season, leaves in various shades of brown and beige. And of school. But with no school to go to, of course. But couldn't she still learn?

"Look Helena. The front is like a yo-yo at the moment. They are all fighting like they are hoping for a miracle." Mother maybe wanted to put her arm around Helena but took her by the hand instead; a firm grip which immediately made Helena straighten up her back, like a schoolgirl. "This is the worst time to be opening a shop, dear. Think of New York. Or London. Or Paris. Ruins."

Mother's grip eased. She let go of her hand.

"Would the front be going across the marketplace?" Mother's hand felt cold, unprotected, she realised. Gloves, she thought. She could do with ordering more gloves. But where from?

"The marketplace?" Mother smiled now, and Helena knew it well, even though she wasn't looking at her face. Her face was the same as her husband's now, she imagined. Like David, Mother always smiled gently whenever she questioned Helena, as if interrogating her made him happy to be a Mother. "I'm planning for after the war, Helena."

"I want to know what's going to happen now. This season, Mother."

"War makes history. It changes fashion, Helena. This you notice every day. But it also kills. It kills old hats, and new hats too."

"You don't understand, Mother." Calm. She needed to stay calm. "All wars end, and then peace ends too. And then we have another war. So why pay any attention? Fashion, weather, style. That's all that counts."

"I'm just being practical, Helena. Stay here. Work for me for another few months. Making films. Together, we'll reinvent porn. You'll see. We'll unite the world, with our porn. Mature porn, for mature men. You are still so pretty, despite being forty, Helena. Especially on the screen. You look better on the screen. Men still like you a lot. In film, they won't touch you. They'll just fantasise about you. It's all right, isn't it? It's not cheating. You are just making some money, for the children. Then, we will see. We might go somewhere. Hawaii?"

"I've always wanted to have a shop, Mother. I've got a family. I'm not enjoying this." She pointed at the kitchen.

"Enjoyment." Mother frowned. "What is joy, or happiness for that matter? Are you enjoying the war?" Mother pointed at the sky, though the window, as if trying to prove to Helena that the war was—after all—as important as the weather. "Look," Mother pointed at a black cloud. "Wars have a certain style. They could be stylish. Porn too. But all wars exhaust themselves and then it's time for a change. Give me the button, I'll sew it on. Give me all of them."

Mother took her hand again, with the buttons inside it, not really to calm her down, or do any sewing, or even to take the buttons from her hand, it seemed, but to stay with her, just stay and be. They were navy blue eyes now, and navy blue buttons, like a deep calm sea, and the grip of her hand felt deep and important too. Her calmness stayed with Helena for a little while. This was an exchange. A transaction.

The buttons felt warm in Helena's fingers. She felt happy she could pay Mother for this moment of calm—with a few warm buttons. Seven, in fact.

But then Helena felt anxious again. It was a trap. Mother was never calm. And Helena could not be calm, with Mother next to her. She had to be cautious. She felt her eyelids tremble a little. "When you mentioned travel—when the war ends—what did you have in mind? A long trip? With a man?"

"No, but there will be three men waiting for you, Helena. Three men pulling you in three different directions as soon as the war ends."

Helena laughed. "This war will never end, Mother."

"It will. And they are just observing you now. But soon enough you'll be the most wanted woman in Hollywood. Look at you. Life is easy with you. Life is beautiful with you. All men ever want is a share of this beauty."

"I am not interested in men. I want to have a shop."

"Men get awfully busy at wartime. Even women start thinking like men, they become men, when they get to my age. I try to do as little as I can. But generally men do get busy. Then, when the war ends, they want to spend time next to a woman who

177

coped well when they were away. The woman who didn't need them. The strongest one. That's what men want in peace—a woman they know can survive a war. A woman who wants nothing from them."

"Is war just to test women?"

"Yes, and your beauty has been tested, Helena. Your beauty is strong. Independent of any men."

"It's true. I want nothing from men. I don't need them."

"That's the most attractive quality in a woman. Her ability to live without any men."

Helena laughed again. "Do you find me attractive, Mother?"

Mother looked at the wall and said: "I am so proud of you, Helena."

Helena entered the bedroom. David was lying in bed looking at the ceiling. "I need you," he said. His raised eyebrows pointed at the attic. He readjusted his hat.

"Take your hat off, David. You're in bed," said Helena.

He touched his head with an expression of disbelief, as if she had just said: "There is a palm tree growing on your head." He then took off his hat, examining it, like an object he had never seen before. The hat was a pure wool beige Trilby, with a little red stain on its brim. She wanted to attribute it to the "secret woman" but couldn't. Was he really seeing her? An affair required organisation and careful planning. It required an agenda. Did David really have one? He couldn't organise himself very well at all! The books he read took over completely. They had so many books; every wall occupied by books. They weren't just his escape.

They were his life. He cared about nothing else. Books and the ideas he found in them. A secret woman made no sense.

"Are the Durands still coming this month?" she asked to change the stream of thoughts in her own head, to direct them to something halfway pleasant.

"Tomorrow. For two or three nights."

They refused to go to the countryside. Somehow, it worked for them. They stayed in town, because they were town people. Not even the Brotherhood would make them move to the countryside.

The Durands were incredibly lucky to be alive. Incredibly lucky to escape any checks, Helena thought. Incredibly lucky to somehow stay invisible, in town, with their heads propped against pillows at night. Often drunk. But not dead. Alive. And maybe alive because they drank.

"I like when they come to stay. They always have so many stories to tell." She never thought of the consequences of course. Anyone hiding the French would immediately be shot in the head, like their next door neighbours. It still didn't seem very real. Not helping friends who need help?

"When they are gone, I need your help, Helena," he said tenderly, so tenderly in fact that she thought that maybe he still loved her.

"How can I help?" It sounded as if she was in the shop already. She might need help too, setting up the shop. This could be a start of a new transaction with her husband. Old, but new.

"Well, there might be a Frenchman coming to live with us."

"A Frenchman? A real Frenchman? An old Frenchman?"

"Not at all. Same age as you and I. An army officer."

An army officer! With a nice hat, no doubt. Father went to Paris once and came back wearing an American Chatham. Ah, Chatham. She thought it was funny then. American Chatham—from Paris. You didn't see any hats around much anymore in Hollywood. They seemed to be replaced by army helmets. And shapeless granny-knitted berets. So clerical! So lacking in chic!

So men could be chic maybe. They had secret lives with secret hats. Affairs.

He was putting the top of his flannel checked pyjamas on, buttoning it up. He had a good chest. With not much hair, but well-shaped and pleasant to touch. Did she ever tell him how good his chest looked? Did the other woman? Like every night, she helped him with the top button.

"Is there something you are not telling me, David?" She felt her fingers tremble as she put the button through the hole. She cared about David. A lot, she realised. She immediately regretted asking, too.

"What do you mean?"

"I mean, a woman. Another woman."

The expression on his face became composed, as if he was able to hide not just one French officer in his attic but a whole army, which he would then organise and send to death. This was the David she didn't know. Not a dreamer but a ruthless king.

"There might be someone else," he said.

"Might?"

"Yes."

"You mean, is there, or not?"

"There might be," he repeated.

She slapped him, hard. Then the other warm cheek. Harder this time.

He laughed, as if her anger was amusing.

Her fists clenched. It felt good to hit him. But at the same time exhausting, every single punch. It hurt her fists to hit him.

She expected him to hit her back but he didn't.

"Stop," he finally said, after several hard punches. "Or I'll call the police."

"The police?"

He laughed again.

There was no police in Hollywood. Army, yes. Militia. But not police.

He just stood there, looking at her, making some kind of decision, or maybe he had decided already, a long time ago.

"Get out," she said.

He took out a box of cigarettes from the pocket in his pyjamas. He passed her a cigarette.

"How angry you are," he said.

A Polish Joke

Do you want to hear a Polish joke? Magda's got a bunch of them. She *loves* Polish jokes. She recently became British but she misses Polish jokes now, she misses them a lot.

This is her first stand up, and she is now in North London, preparing, looking over her script, at home, with a cup of English tea. The performance is in a few days. They never saw a Polish stand-up comedian before, in a busy pub, she doesn't think. Polish jokes have accompanied Magda all her life, she will explain, up until she left Poland as a Polack, Polak, *or* Polka, to be accurate. Please, don't laugh, she will ask. Just listen. This is a conference on Polish jokes, this is not stand-up. It's serious.

Polak, in Polish, means a Polish man, and it does not have the conno-
tation of being stupid. Polak sounds good, and proud. Polka means
a Polish woman, hence polka dots perhaps, on Polka's dress? Polka
is proud too, and not stupid either. Not to other Poles. Not when she
resides in Poland. It was only when I travelled West that I became
labelled as stupid, and a Polak—a Polish man in fact—even if I
behaved wisely and very lady-like.

She'll need to cut some of that. Too much information maybe. Too many definitions. Not snappy enough. As a Brit, even a Polish Brit, Magda finds it strange not to be laughed at by other nationalities, very strange, she will explain. Polish jokes kept her so alert maybe. And now, she is laughing at these jokes, laughing in English, with the Brits, holding her British passport which cost her two thousand pounds, but it's not the same as being laughed at. She often wonders: How many years, generations, and light years will need to pass before she is asked:

Question: Why don't British women use their vibrators too much?
Answer: Because it chips their teeth!

Nobody will laugh. It's understandable. It's rude AND sexist AND racist AND, as it's usually told, it's a Polish joke.

Laughing at nationalities and women, like Polish women, is no longer
fashionable of course. But maybe in the future, say by 2075, things
will have changed.

This line sort of escapes her, every time. She repeats this twice now, so that she doesn't forget. And then the rest of the script doesn't make sense. She sips her English tea. The tea is almost cold, but she doesn't mind. She is still a little Polish in that way. If nationalities still exist, in 2075, then maybe Polish men will find a reason to rudely say: *Look at these British women!* And if women are still a separate gender from men in 2075, then Polish men will maybe tease them in what will be a fashionable way, post-sexist way, in fact:

Question: Why do all British women stick highly sophisticated vibrators in their mouths? This is not where highly sophisticated vibrators normally go, is it?
Answer: Maybe there is something wrong with these women? Maybe they like their teeth chipped?

Hearing this answer, British women will get offended and sometimes cry, Magda will say. But maybe by 2075, British women will no longer pay any attention to men, even Polish men.

And what shall she wear? Just jeans and a T-shirt? She looks at another page, and then checks herself in the mirror. It will be OK. They don't have to laugh, of course not. The script is getting denser, with fewer paragraph breaks now. Will the world ever laugh at British men, collectively, the way they laughed at Polish men in the twentieth century? Will the world see them as not only stupid but also drunk, like in the Polish joke that goes:

Question: Why do you drink vodka, Daddy? It tastes so bitter! It's awful, in fact!

Answer: I drink it for this very reason, Son. Sometimes in life you just grind your teeth and drink your vodka. It's called "assuming responsibility." You do it every minute of your life. Shot after shot. But I also drink it because your mother keeps sticking her vibrator in her mouth, and it's chipped up her teeth very badly.

So who is this Polish man from the Polish joke who drinks all the time and has an ugly wife with chipped teeth? She will ask. He is, first of all, quite stupid. He is as stupid as a Polish woman, and a lot less clever than a white man or a black man. He seems to lack practical skills, and—unlike a white man or a black man—he doesn't know how to survive in a desert.

She needs an example here. An example of a good joke. She makes a note. The margin is all red now, with her tight red handwriting.

You see, there's a white man, a black man, and a Polak. They are going to the desert to be contestants on the Survivor TV Show and can take one item each. Someone asks the very clever white man: "What will you take?" He replies: "Water, so I can drink when I'm thirsty." Then this person asks a clever black guy. He says he'll take a sandwich to eat when he is hungry. Finally the Polak is asked the same question, and the Polak, because he is stupid as fuck, says: "I'll take a car door to the desert, in case it's hot. I can roll the window down. And then I won't be hot."

This Polak is not white. He is just a Polak colour. He is stupid. He also likes to fuck animals, especially chickens! Magda must say it louder. Maybe she will clap her hands in the air here too. Not white!

Ah, this one is good too. She just remembered. Red pen, between two lines now, in very small caps:

Question: Why did the Polak cross the road?
Answer: He couldn't get his huge Polish dick out of the chicken.

And did you know that when a Polak has a hard-on, he thinks it's a health condition? She laughs to herself now. This is funny. Funny to her.

Question: Why did the Polack put ice in his condom?
Answer: To keep the swelling down.

And then, out of nowhere, she hears this line, a voice, in her head, like another old joke:

Did you ever hear the one about the Polack who falls in love? And not just with chickens but with a fellow Polish woman? Or just a woman. Any woman. A woman he likes.

Magda adds this to the script, with the red pen. She relaxes. Closes her eyes.

Once, he met a Polish girl at a disco, in Gdynia, in December, 2075. He almost fucked her in the gents' toilet but then they just ended up talking. They had a nice little conversation about her mum. Her mum was sick. She was very sick, in fact. The Polack really wanted to fuck the Polish girl but because of her sick mum, he also wanted to give it time, too. He told her this. So they just talked, which was unusual for Polish people. And then, just like that, he was stupidly in love.

He then went back to his little mountain village called Zakopane. It was a nice place, full of chicken fuckers and women with chipped teeth, but the Polack missed the girl. He missed Gdynia, too. He missed the Baltic Sea. But it was her. Her he missed the most. He often talked to her on Skype, and once, when she talked, just talked about her dying mother, he started touching himself. He asked not to switch the camera on. He touched himself a little, and he was glad she didn't want the camera on but he told her about touching himself anyway.

"Sometimes my hard-on seems like a health condition. Like it's a bit uncomfortable. Like I should maybe try and put some ice in my condom."

The girl laughed. He loved the way she laughed. He loved to make her laugh.

"You are so funny and wise," she said. "I feel you are there, all for me. You listen."

"Yes," he said, and then he came. He came into his fist. She didn't know of course. He didn't make a sound. He just went a bit quiet.

"If you and I went to a desert, like the Sahara, what would you take with you?" she asked.

"Nothing," he said. And then he changed his mind and said: "I'd take condoms, and ice. Or maybe just a man pill. And more ice. Also my pet chicken, to eat and fuck, and car doors, and polka-dot dresses, for you, but really for me. To undress you with."

She laughed. She told him she had a vibrator. All Gdynia girls owned a vibrator, often with fifty-seven settings. Of course. It was the year 2075 and vibrators were better than the real thing.

"I don't like technology, though. I'm scared of it," she said.

"Technology won't hurt you," he said. "It could improve your life. It could even be fun, I am sure. Maybe ask a friend. You know. A girlfriend."

In 2075, everybody was declared bisexual, so the Polack was worried she might suddenly want to be with a woman, but he hoped not, at least, not for long.

"Would you ever help me?" she asked.

"I don't know. I'd rather help myself. To you."

She laughed. She said she would think of him, if she ever used technology.

His fist was wet again.

The following week she told him that her mum died. She wanted him at the funeral.

"Of course," he said. She cried and cried and it felt so good to hear her cry. It felt to him like a release, like the closest thing to her coming, and he hoped he could make her feel better straight away but he knew he couldn't make it better; it was her mum, he was sorry. He couldn't fix it for her, even in 2075, so he listened and imagined her just crying on his shoulder. Crying a lot. But also using a vibrator. Technology. Putting it into her mouth. Just doing anything. Anything to make her laugh, and not cry.

The next day he sent her flowers. Tulips. Black tulips. It was springtime and tulips were just nice flowers, especially these black tulips. They seemed larger than regular tulips.

That night she asked him if his dick was big. He didn't know what to say. He was tall, and everything about him was long, so maybe long. Yes. But big? He could show her, on Skype. They could have sex on Skype. Like, real sex. But they were not ready to do it remotely. They were not ready to do it skin to skin. He felt like a knob talking about his dick to her. He wanted his Polack dick to speak for himself. One day. Soon.

Gdynia was beautiful in springtime, everything seemed a different shade of blue, like there were suddenly more blues and greens than in wintertime, less traffic, fewer people.

She picked him up in a little Fiat full of chickens.

She was wearing a black veil over her face and a black miniskirt. Black knee-high boots. In 2075, people no longer pretended sex and death were not part of the same thing, thank God.

"She was British," she said suddenly, in the car. "A British woman," she said, both lowering her voice and laughing, as if it was a joke.

He didn't want to make jokes about British women. He didn't agree with them. But then, he thought, maybe it was actually appropriate. Maybe it will help her. It will cheer her up.

"My grandparents had a British hoover," he told her. "A good hoover. It hoovered well."

She laughed. Ah, how she laughed. He wanted to be inside her before he kissed her. He wanted to say hello with his dick, and then kiss, and then shake hands, say hello, many times, many ways. Just fuck her, as if she was his sister, as if she was a Polack, oh, she was a Polack! How stupid of him!

"Is that all you know about Britain? You just know their hoovers?"

"Yes, I am afraid so. I always wanted to go but it just seemed so *far. And you know. It's a funny old place. Britain."*

"Yes. My mum was nice though. You know, she was actually quite funny. They sometimes have a good sense of humour. The Brits, I mean"

"Do they? I'm glad. Was she nice? She wasn't too rough on you? Not too strict?"

"No, she was actually lovely. Really, really nice. Exceptionally nice, and kind. One of a kind. Almost like us."

"That's good." He was glad. Glad her mum was nice, and not rough, or unkind. It was important, even if she was now dead. Even if he never met her. What a shame he never met her, or fucked her, if she was so nice. What a shame she had to die.

He looked at this girl, his girl soon, he imagined, and in a slightly new light. If her mum was British then she was not just Polish. She was also half-British. So maybe, maybe sex first, before the first kiss. He didn't know why he was thinking this, or why this was important, but it was, and he was honest with himself at least. With a Polish girl he would not even consider this in real life but now. Yes. He wanted to do it. With her. Maybe he just felt physical, more physical, suddenly. She must like sex. She must like it a lot. All the time. Never enough for him, or too much. And love? Love can be part of sex, or not. He would see how it goes, where it takes them, how it comes and goes.

The priest was too drunk, or too stupid, or just forgot to come. Or maybe by 2075, there were no more priests left in Poland. Nobody else came to the funeral either. No brothers or sisters, or even the neighbours. They must have hated her so much. Or were just busy fucking each other, or fucking chickens?

So they buried the mother themselves, on their hands and knees, digging dirt with their fingernails. But first, they took off all her jewellery, all her rings off her fingers. They had to cut off one finger in order to do that. And then, on top of the grave, exhausted, the Polack just lifted up his girl's miniskirt. She had no underpants on of course, so it was easy. His dick felt so huge. It was all that mattered. All he could feel now. His huge Polack dick. Hugely in love.

"What are you waiting for?"

And he answered, "I don't know. I just can't. I know this is perfect, with death and everything, we could even dig your mum up again, for later, but I just can't. I want to be on Skype. Love you on Skype. It's like, longing is my natural setting. It's my happy place. Can we find Skype?"

She just stared at his hand now, it seemed, or maybe beyond it, past it, through her own fingers. As if recording it for later, with her eyes, with her breathing, and not breathing, with the fingers. This little memory of his fingers almost touching her fingers; her little dirty fucking Polack fingers.

I wish to thank: A.M. Bakalar; Michael Tate, Jack Coling and everyone at Jantar Publishing; Paul Maliszewski; Scott Bradfield; Zoë Fairbairns, Martina Evans, Conor Montague, Susanna Babington, Kit Habianic, Shere Ross, Geri Dogmetchi, May Al-Issa, Rachel Joseph, Pippa Moss, Karen Mullen and all the writers I met at City Lit; Magda Raczyńska and the Polish Cultural Institute in London; Jeremy Osborne and Karen Rose of Sweet Talk Productions; Liz Hoggard, Jan Krasnowolski, Wioletta Greg, Rosie Goldsmith, Anna Błasiak, Maria Jastrzębska, Jakub Krupa, Alicia Clyde, and Emily Hall. Marta Dziurosz and Free Word Centre; Marta Sordyl and Poles Connect; Harriet Williams and the British Council. Amy Swales and *Stylist* online. Paweł Dembowski and Marcin Zwierzchowski at *Nowa Fantastyka*. Gabriella Bello, Yüksel Adıgüzel and Gary Neale. My cousin Rafał Rutkowski and Teatr Montownia. Finally, my parents Anna and Aleksander and my sister Ewa Surażyńska. Dziękuję!

Also available from Jantar Publishing

CHILDREN OF OUR AGE
by A.M. Bakalar

Karol and his wife are the rising stars of the Polish community in London but Karol is a ruthless entrepreneur whose fortune is built on the backs of his fellow countrymen. The Kulesza brothers, mentally unstable Igor and his violent brother Damian, dream about returning to Poland one day. A loving couple, Mateusz and Angelika, believe against all odds that good things will happen to people like them. Gradually, all of these lives become dramatically entwined, and each of them will have to decide how far they are willing to go in pursuit of their dreams.

THREE PLASTIC ROOMS
by Petra Hůlová

Translated from the Czech by Alex Zucker

A foul-mouthed Prague prostitute muses on her profession, aging and the nature of materialism. She explains her world view in the scripts and commentaries of her own reality TV series combining the mundane with fetishism, violence, wit and an unvarnished mixture of vulgar and poetic language.

www.jantarpublishing.com

Also available from Jantar Publishing

IN THE NAME OF THE FATHER AND OTHER
STORIES
by Balla

Translated from the Slovak by Julia & Peter Sherwood

Balla is often described as 'the Slovak Kafka' for his depictions of the
absurd and the mundane. *In the Name of the Father* features a nameless
narrator reflecting on his life, looking for someone else to blame for
his failed relationship with his parents and two sons, his serial adultery,
the breakup of his marriage and his wife's descent into madness.

BURYING THE SEASON
by Antonín Bajaja

Translated from the Czech by David Short

An affectionate, multi-layered account of small town life in central
Europe beginning in the early 1930s and ending in the 21st Century.
Adapting scenes from Fellini's *Amarcord*, Bajaja's meandering narrative
weaves humour, tragedy and historical events into a series of compelling
nostalgic anecdotes.

www.jantarpublishing.com

Also available from Jantar Publishing

BLISS WAS IT IN BOHEMIA
by Michal Viewegh

Translated from the Czech by David Short

A wildly comic story about the fate of a Czech family from the 1960s
onwards. At turns humorous, ironic and sentimental, an engaging
portrait of their attempts to flee from history (meaning the 1968
Soviet invasion of Czechoslovakia) – or at least to ignore it as long as
possible... Light-hearted and sophisticated at once, this is a book that
reminds us that comedy can tackle large historical subjects successfully.

GRAVELARKS
by Jan Křesadlo

Translated from the Czech by Václav Z J Pinkava

Zderad, a noble misfit, investigates a powerful party figure in 1950s
Czechoslovakia. His struggle against blackmail, starvation and betrayal
leaves him determined to succeed where others have failed and
died. Set in Stalinist era Central Europe, *GraveLarks* is a triumphant
intellectual thriller navigating the fragile ambiguity between sado-
masochism, black humour, political satire, murder and hope.

www.jantarpublishing.com

Also available from Jantar Publishing

THREE FACES OF AN ANGEL
by Jiří Pehe

Translation by Gerald Turner
Foreword by Dr Marketa Goetz-Stankiewicz, FRSC

Three Faces of an Angel is a novel about the twentieth century that
begins when time was linear and ended when the notion of progress
was less well defined. The Brehmes' story guides the reader through
revolution, war, the holocaust, and ultimately exile and return. A
novel about what man does to man and whether God intervenes.

KYTICE
CZECH & ENGLISH BILINGUAL EDITION
by Karel Jaromír Erben

Translation and Introduction by Susan Reynolds

Kytice was inspired by Erben's love of Slavonic myth and the folklore
surrounding such creatures as the Noonday Witch and the Water
Goblin. First published in 1853, these poems, along with Mácha's Máj
and Němcová's Babička, are the best loved and most widely read 19th
century Czech classics. Published in the expanded 1861 version, the
collection has moved generations of artists and composers, including
Dvořák, Smetana and Janáček.

www.jantarpublishing.com